www.themuseandthemechanism.com

www.pretendgenius.com

The Muse and the Mechanism

Josh Davis

PretendGeniusPress

London, New York, San Francisco, Seattle, Washington D.C.

PretendGeniusPress
www.pretendgenius.com

ISBN 0-9747261-7-6

Printed in the United States of America

tracklist:

the setup, 1
the impossible lightness of breathing, 13
the weekend odyssey, 25
le sommeil se prolonge, 45
zen girls and the hieroglyphs, 61
epicureanism at work, 71
like dreaming up from a wake, 109
time and distance, 127
the deafening indifference, 143
intermission, 153
a life in letters, 161
perspective, 175
ethan and oxycodone, 185
everybody has been burned, 191
a show about nothing, 219
after the flood, 227

"I've been a miner for a heart of gold"
-Neil Young

chapter one:

The Setup.

I wake up. The clock is blinking 12:00.

Lola is asleep at my side. I run my fingers across her exposed skin.

The pillows all smell like her hair. They are especially soft and warm, as if they've just come out of the dryer. The sheets and blankets smell like her skin— like fruit and soap and sweat.

It's strange to miss a person that's lying right next to you.

There's a dent in my ceiling in the shape of James Christopher. Last week he nearly fell through the attic floor following a series of accidental dives down the stairs.

The dent has two legs and an L-shaped body. I match the outline to Lola's inanimate curves.

An hour later, she finally stirs.

"What time is it?"

"I haven't set the clock…"

She glances at a little plastic watch that's attached to her handbag.

"Shit. I'll be back…" she mumbles as she kisses me goodbye with her morning mouth.

By now I've memorized her entire routine. First, she'll get into the car and put on an old Pavement or Cat Power song. After the two mile drive home, she'll march directly into the shower where a thousand strange soaps are waiting, strategically positioned, as if there were actually a soap made for each square inch of her small, frail body. Next she'll disperse said soaps through a series of sponges, damp cloths and long sheets of coarse, stretchy polyester. Soapy skin sanded and soaked by sad stretched-out squares.

Her eyes will be lifeless and unromantic—like a soldier marching, or assembling a firearm.

Next she'll pull up a little red mirror, squint her eyes, and begin applying makeup to every visible part of her body.

Following this, she'll tend to a large narcissistic cat who scratches at company.

Finally, she'll choke down an entire Tupperware container of week old lasagna, securing herself something to complain about later.

This is the way it is for 13 days out of each month. Lola and the Cuban missile crisis are forever joined in unholy matrimony. Not that I'm much more exciting. I spend most of my life remembering things.

Today I lay in bed remembering the night the dent was born.

James came home from his usual bar after a particularly uneventful night and immediately liberated two beers from the fridge. He then stumbled to a nearby couch, drank the first beer, and vomited it back up into his lap.

Next, he drank the second and stumbled into the kitchen for another.

Following this, he lurched his way out to the front porch for a smoke. I walked out after him to watch his blinking eyes, and feet that slowly sway like thin trees in a stiff wind. But he tipped over just as I opened the door.

James then got up, seemingly unphased by the glass bottle that broke his fall, and crawled upstairs with two more beers tucked under his arm.

A minute later he fell back down said stairs, muttered something unintelligible, straightened himself out, and walked into the kitchen for another.

I tried to hold him off, but he only writhed and

shouted, "Goddammit Fell! Whateryou, my fucking father? Leggo!"

I let go.

James crawled back up the stairs on his belly, stood up, tripped over his TV, and sent its cousin the VCR dangling over the stairwell, hanging on only by its long black umbilical cord.

At this point Stephen staggered out of bed to find the source of the noise. James obliged by falling down on cue.

Before we could help him, he pulled himself up, winked at us, and tripped through the hallway for another beer.

Stephen called after him, "James? James—why don't you just sleep down here, man?"

"What? Naw. Naw, I'm alright. I gotta test tomorrah."

"What does that have to do with anything?"

"Let him go, man. His liver's on autopilot."

"What the fuck did he drink?"

"As far as I can tell, he challenged the entire Russian parliament…"

"Damned commies!"

"Well, at least he can hear us."

"Yeah, watch this…"

James lay down on his stomach and slithered upstairs.

"He'll go to sleep now for sure," Stephen said grimly, "don't worry."

Stephen and I stepped outside for a cigarette just as James's battered body barreled back down the stairs. His head lodged against door, trapping us outside until he regained consciousness several minutes later and stumbled back into the kitchen.

The next day James swore off drinking for good. The next night he forgot.

I up and shower. The bathroom window looks out into a field of frost in the back yard. All the cars are covered in sharp crystalline stars. Even the road is coated in a thin black sheet. Nothing's moving. It's as if the frost has frozen time.

I walk out to find Lola sitting in the living room wearing a winter frown and army-green pants that appear painted on. Her eyes are as silver and dead as the air outside.

Lola wasn't always like this. She used stay up all night playing guitar, or making sculptures out of the crème containers they give you in 24-hour diners, or writing poems about the children who wait in line at McDonalds. She used to collect words. I remember the day she learned the word vitriolic. It was a good word—not one of those a and b words like abominate, abstruse anathema, atrophy, arcane, beleaguered, bemused, or brindled. Vitriolic comes later, is more mature, and has a nice roll, "riolic." She was so proud of that word.

Now she just eats, sleeps, pouts, and watches endless hours of Animal Planet.

We walk a few hundred yards to a sandwich shop where Stephen paces blankly behind a glass case of bagels and exotic breads.

He manages to sneak us a few sandwiches and motions for Lola to pocket a couple of bottled coffee drinks from a nearby display. His eyes are silver as well. They carry all the weight and contradiction of the clashing seasons.

A week ago we'd have found Althea at his side smiling as beautifully blank as a child. She would squeak and laugh and giggle and gesture, and her eyes would light a bright blue spark in your belly. She was fearless in her innocence. She was the only thing keeping Stephen from dealing again.

But she fled home abruptly for the semester break, told Stephen she, "really needed to find herself," and quickly exited his life.

After that he stayed in his room for days, sulking, dead, and weeping for the void, or for that last light of childhood finally gone dark.

Six months prior, Stephen pulled into the driveway after a long days work, not noticing the sirens flashing in the backyard. In fact, he didn't notice anything out of the ordinary at all until they cuffed him to the car.

They had already been inside. They had already gashed the couches and confiscated a number of bags, pill bottles, razors, weights, and scales.

I moved in a month later.

Something in Stephen seemed to soften after the raid reduced his career options. Now, if not for his 6'2" frame, shaved head, angry slit eyes and axiom goatee, you would swear he is no less than a beleaguered saint.

The frost cannot begin to express the cold outside. Imagine standing inside a freezer—naked—and turning a fan on. Imagine a cold so sharp it feels like jagged metal.

We walk back across the frozen ground, through the frozen air, and under the pale grey clouds that hover over us like ominous ice cubes.

The wind blows from west to east to south and back to west. It sweeps drunkenly about us, hitting us from all sides, marking every inch of exposed skin with its sharp currents.

Back at the house, Lola and I concede to the couch to complain aloud our boredom over the gentle lullaby of television. We are in this mannequin generation together. We are in these glass and metal futures. Our chairs and mouse pads are more comfortable than our beds. The television is more comfortable than our heads. We are in this together.

Stephen walks in a good while later mid-laugh, with a girl and a six-pack of beer.

He pulls me quickly aside.
"Remember that girl I told you about?"
"Yeah—is that her?"
"Yeah. Look—that's Althea's best friend."
"Jesus," I cover my eyes to laugh. "You fucking moron…"
"I know…I know. But I'm going to be good tonight Charlie. I swear. I'm going to be good. I have to. I'll never get her back if I fuck this up…"
"You want me to… try to keep you in line?"
"Yeah…please?"
Lola overhears us and pulls Stephen into my room, playfully scribbling be good in bold letters on the palm of his right hand. She downs one of his beers on her way out the door, singing, "I'll be back…"

A minute later, James's girl bursts in looking a little flustered. She smiles unevenly and runs up the stairs. None of us seem at all alarmed.
Then something crashes overhead, and the girl quickly reappears. She speaks with an uneven stutter like she's trying too hard to sound like she's been

paying attention, or like a half-full glass aiming at three quarters.

"Hey Charlie—I got some mid-grade. Wanna go for a ride?"

Stephen nods that it's all right. I turn my head uneasily at him, but agree anyway. "I'll be back…"

My car is covered in silver frost and street dust. I scrape off a thin layer, kick the engine on, and head toward the quieter, safer sections of town. Five miles of back roads easily erase the slums and the aimless kids marching down the beer-glass brown streets.

A swift left and we're through the iron gates and into rows of neatly sculpted boxwoods and BMWs, where even the poor can become invisible at night in smoky automobiles.

The girl squeaks, "so James confessed last night. He told me he's been seeing some bartender-chick. Then he fell into the wall, bounced off the fridge, and hit the ground face-first."

"A little drunk, huh?"

"Yeah, I think."

"Man—why do you even put up with him? You come over, bring food, do his dishes, clean his room, have sex with him and leave. I mean—you're the perfect woman…"

She only smiles. She thinks she's playing as many games with him as he is with her. But James always seems to win. He always outsmarts her. She doesn't realize that the only chance she's got is to outlast his liver.

Her eyes get glassy for a minute. Everything is covered in sharp crystalline stars. Nothing's moving.

When she speaks again her voice becomes vastly different. She sounds hopeful and naïve—child-like, honest, real.

"So there's this other guy—my ex-boyfriend—I saw him yesterday…"

"Oh yeah?"

"Yeah. He's great. He used to make me things. Actual, real, fucking honest things. Sweet things. Like—he made me this." She holds up a wrist wrapped in a homemade bracelet. "He has this innocence about him. The other night, I made a pass at him, and he wouldn't even touch me! Imagine that."

She pauses and smiles inside an invisible circle of light.

"Then leave. Stop playing games with barflies and fucking leave. There's no reason to waste when there's wonder. Leave…"

Her eyes are glassy again.

I hop out of the car, high, and bound back into the house. Stephen is sitting on the couch flipping through channels and beers while danger sits on a neighboring sofa.

Lola is spread out on the floor in my bedroom giving marching orders to computerized armies.

I make a couple of drinks by combining the bottoms of several bottles into an awful brown confection. I hand one to the polite phantom, and one to Stephen who's been busy sliding slowly from couch to floor.

"Low—d`you want one?"

"NO! Nomore!" Between the cannon fire I can hear the end of her laughter.

Stephen and the girl are still reclined safely in the recesses of their respective couches. I retreat to room, open a book, and pretend to read. Lola's eyes barely leave the screen.

I don't notice Stephen as he slips into his room. I don't notice the girl following him inside.

Lola notices. She catches him skipping towards the kitchen for another round of beers. "Stephen!" she whispers, "be good!"

Stephen winks and disappears. The door locks behind him.

"We tried."

Ten minutes later, the girl rushes out, mortified. She dashes out the front door, slamming it shut hard as if to emphasize the finality.

Stephen slumps into the hall.

"I really fucked up."

"What happened?"

"Nothing—nothing good. I—I stopped in the middle though…at least…" He looks at me now. "Jesus, I really fucked up."

Stephen ponders his pack of smokes.

"Let's have one."

"Yeah——yeah."

We walk outside. I know the distance. I remember.

"I don't know. I gotta get out of here."

Stephen paces the yard with one hand on his cigarette and the other on his head. His eyes are silver and dead. "I really fucked up."

I'm silent. I'm searching for something real, something honest to say.

I could say it hurts, that I know, that I remember. I could tell him that it's natural to be lost for a while afterward. I could tell him that I know the feeling—that I know it's like being in the middle of an ocean—and there's no horizon but sea, and there is no sun, and there are no stars. There is only that bright blinding clarity that is no clarity. There is only the fog that is the truth.

Or I could just talk—say something.

"I think—I think that this bothers you is good. It shows you've grown. Man—you used to jack cars, rob, steal, sell, use. But you left all that. Now you're getting used to goodness and it's fucking hard. I know. It's almost a revelation to feel real fear."

"Yeah. I know." He pauses and looks at the frost. "I'm going away for a while Charlie. I need some time to figure everything out. Everything's—different. I need some time..."

I give Stephen my car knowing it offers some insurance that he'll be all right. It's good to tear down the walls every now and then. I know. It's good as long as you leave the door.

I think he'll be all right to drive. I think he'll be all right. It's good to tear down the walls.

Lola sits, stunned, watching us in the hallway. She's talking to herself. "He winked at me and then..."

Stephen only mumbles, "I...I don't know..."

I watch him drive away. I think he'll be alright.

James comes in soon after, wildly drunk and running into walls that aren't there. He trips over the exposed speaker wire in the living room and stumbles into the hall.

I don't recognize the girl he's with. She's tall and cocky like him. Her laughter is deep. Her speech is only a little less slurred than his.

The refrigerator shakes ajar, and I hear the crisp sound of a beer can bending open. kkkcchhehhh!

James stumbles into my room.

"Caaan Iborrah—pieceapaper? Some—somethngtawrite with?" He scribbles a note and staples it to the door:

Gone out. Having fun.

And he disappears in a fit of laughter.

An hour later his girl comes in with the widest grin you've ever seen.

"Hellooo," she says, waiting for our reading of the obvious.

"Damn woman, you are downright glowing."

"Yeah, well, I—I ran into an old friend."

"I take it it went well."

"Yeah. Well," laughing, "yeah…hey—can I borrow a pen?"

She writes over James's scribbling:

Having more fun! HA ha ha ha ha.

And then she disappears, giddy, glowing and obvious.

Now the house is empty save for Lola and I, and I have to make another drink to kill the quiet.

At five a.m. James stumbles in uncomfortably, holding on to the walls for balance. From the other room I can hear the crumpling of paper.

I look in. He's fumbling with the phone in the living room.

He dials slowly. The long rings hang hard in the empty air.

Ten minutes later, the front door creaks open.

The groan of the gate is followed by the heavy sound of four feet clomping upstairs, and later by the repetitious thud of late night laborious sex.

I wake up somewhat jealous of the drunk who can charm the decency out of a woman. But more than that, I want his girl gone. I want her weakness away from me. I want no more reminders of how easy it is to fold. I want no more evidence of how simple it is to forget who we are or of the effortlessness in which youth falls asleep inside the first thing it sees. Maybe I don't have any strength of my own anymore. But I certainly don't need anyone else there to remind me.

I walk outside to see my car really gone.
And maybe I envy Stephen the most, who still has the legs to run.

All the cars are covered in sharp crystalline stars. Even the road is coated in a thin black sheet. Nothing's moving. It's as if the frost has frozen time.

Lola is asleep inside.

I am in the street now looking down the open length of road that runs through the horizon. I am in the street thinking how far this life does stretch, and what little courage it would take to walk.

chapter two:

The Impossible Lightness of Breathing.

Alton opens on a long highway dotted with fruit stands and wheat fields. Further in there are grey houses with white shutters, blue houses with white shutters, brick houses, yellow houses, and little green houses with white shutters. Tiny wooden men sit on modest wooden poles and plywood horses in the front lawn. Beside them are their good friends the flamingo, and occasionally, the daring red wooden tulip.

Soon there are gas stations, convenience stores, fast food restaurants, all night diners, and a tattoo parlor.

Off to the right is the newly restored downtown area where old brick hardware stores, court houses, and law offices still stand. Behind these there are marble and silver banks, upscale art galleries, coffee shops, hair salons, antique furniture stores, and fashionably overpriced taverns.

In the center is a long cobblestone walkway lined with red Japanese Maple trees, bricked in bushes and flower arrangements, hot dog vendors, permit park benches, and expensive apartment houses.

Off to the left are the slums, complete with bus station, thrift stores, old warehouses, barbed wire, a mining pit, a fleet of prehistoric black barges floating on oily water, and a shimmering silver refinery. Old one story houses with rusted-out, immovable cars line the streets. Kids with cans of soda and pockets of nickel candy ride bikes by abandoned building sites, and old men trace the railroad tracks with paper bags.

Straight ahead is Route 13, which splits the town in two and is marked at each end by a Wal-Mart. 13 North is home to several malls, Movie Theaters, giant hardware stores and upscale restaurant chains. 13 South houses the college and a number of bars and fast food eateries.

West down the highway is the city park where Sunday summer orchestras used to play concertos to crowds of elderly aficionados and their forever squirming grandchildren. Further up is the Alton zoo, complete with bison, ocelots, ostriches, leopards, ground hogs, two alligators, several snakes, three Kodiak bears and any number of squawking tropical birds.

The rest of the town splits into a V, where the slums and schools settle in the stomach, and the upper-class communities with gates and waterways line the arms.

I live in the center, a hundred yards from a grocery store, fifty from a bar, a quarter mile to two more, and just across the street from a pizza parlor and all night gas station. All in all—not a bad location for $200 a month.

James lives upstairs in his beer bottles and holes. Stephen—had he been back—would be across the hall, sitting shirtless at his computer and listening to techno. He walks around the house all day like that— with slopping beer belly hanging out in the open, belching and farting, and leaving a trail of stale pizza crusts wherever he goes.

I'm sitting in my room reading by the window overlooking the empty driveway.

How To Disappear Completely

I sit on my bed for long periods of time listening to my heart beat, or else watching that L-shape in the ceiling, waiting for it to do something spectacular. It just sits there, staring at me.

The crust has almost fallen off. The roof has almost caved. There is a feeling of suspended animation. I live in that L-shape. I hang by the crust of old, rotten wood.

Nothing happens.

The house is bitter and empty without Stephen. His room doesn't chirp or click or buzz with the usual music. His friends aren't shouting at each other in the hallway.

Some do come or call or wonder where he's gone. "Family emergency," I tell them, "he'll be gone for at least a week." They just nod, turn around, and fly off in their souped-up yellow sports cars carrying their baggy orange pants to the next house.

The attic is quiet as well. James has been at his mother's house "doing laundry" for three days now. I'm not really even sure what that means.

I sit on my bed for long periods of time listening to my heart beat. I'm not sure if it's off or not. Sometimes it seems to beat harder for just a pulse or two, and then my chest rattles and I remember to breathe. Sometimes it beats like it wants out.

It's Friday night. All my friends are a quarter mile away at a karaoke bar laughing at a tall, thin, white-shirted, half-bearded, balding, gangly crooner who ruins Rolling Stones songs and often does even disco harm. We named him "Waldo" after his red and white striped shirts and Wonder Years glasses. We love Waldo. Waldo, to us, is the last proper absurd, kicking six-year-old on the planet.

I eventually give in and walk across the street, through the grocery store parking lot, and past the pool of renegade ducks that live by the train tracks. They quack at me obtusely as I pass. I yell at them that ducks shouldn't be out so late in such a disreputable neighborhood.

Inside the bar, Eve, Tim and the others down beers by a table in the back. In the front, a father and son are singing and rapping back bad heavy metal lyrics. They sound even whiter than the assholes that wrote this song.

To my left is a field of faces from high school. There's the jock that used to copy answers in English class. There's the kid with long hair who cut it off and became cool. There's the girl that I always meant to talk to. There are the girls that everyone always meant to talk to.

I think we develop courage last. I think we are born, breathe, crawl, walk, talk, play video games, do long division, speak foreign languages, bat .400, learn Beethoven's Fifth on the coronet, climb mount Everest, read Paradise Lost six times, and then learn how to ask a girl out for coffee.

Waldo jumps up next and sings Satisfaction in a cracking forty-year-old pubescent voice while doing cartwheels and dancing with the wait staff.

I order a beer and join my friends in the back. Henry, James Watson, Jude, Timothy, and Sid all stand around Eve doing impressions and buying her drinks. Eve is tall for a woman, 21 and slender with long brown hair, striking grey-blue eyes, and a heavy bottom lip that pouts with more regularity than a postman. She never dates any of us, but we don't seem to mind. At least we never stop trying.

"Charlie, hey!" she sings as she wraps herself around me drunkenly.

"What the hell's going on?"

"Well—let me tell you—it's dollar Corona night, and…"

"Ahh."

"Yeeeah."

"Charlie!"

I shake hands and grin at everyone. They've all got a few hours head start and seem to be walking around in some sort of quicksand.

Tim is especially lead-footed. He's smiling like a kid in a candy store on acid, and laughing uncontrollably about everything around him.

"What's up Fell?"

"Not much…"

"Have you seen Christopher?"

"Not in a few days."

"Didn't he fall through the ceiling?"

"Almost."

"That's funny."

"Sure."

"How does anybody fall through the ceiling?"

"Very carefully."

"What an idiot."

"We all have our moments."

"He almost fell through…"

He starts telling everyone else. Then he tells me to tell everyone else. Then something else comes up.

"Remember the time…"

One of the girls that I always meant to talk to is onstage singing a Madonna song. Her cartoon brown eyes flash and her hips drift hypnotically from side to side. James, Henry, Jude and I are transfixed.

"Didn't we go to school with her?"

"Yeah. She was in my algebra two class."

"No shit?"

"No shit."

"You ever talk to her."

"Nope. But I used to sit behind her. She used to wear these shorts…"

"Damn…"

People clap but no one claps differently. In the movies, someone always gets up and blows everyone away with their stunning note for note rendition of a Celine Dion Warwick song. In real life, we're all just here to look at each other and get shit-faced. No one but your friends gives a damn what you sound like, and even they clap the same for all their friends.

Sid gets up next and screams his way through Nine Inch Nail's "Closer." We cheer wildly, but only because he gets to say fuck six times in a public place.

I don't notice my heartbeat anymore, and order Coronas until I've caught up.

I leave a little before closing time and stumble back by the obtuse ducks and the grocery store, past another bar and through a row of street lights and small yellow houses with white shutters.

The bed is happy to see me. The ceiling spins, "hello." I scratch a little red spot on my stomach and laugh. Tim, ducks, Eve, Gangly, Dion Warwick, Long Division—

In the morning I feel feverish and the little red spot has multiplied and spread across my stomach. I look my new friends in the mirror and become light-headed.

I vomit whatever I forgot to eat yesterday and heave whatever I didn't.

The floor is cool and the ceiling spins, "hello."

I lay there and shiver for a while. I've had chicken pox. It isn't poison ivy. I've been inoculated for everything else. I think.

My throat is swollen and red. I pour a few handfuls of water over my face and stumble back into bed.

When I wake up, the spots are still there. I'd call the doctor, but she'd only tell me I was dying. My face flushes with blood and my hearts beats faster.

Tim calls an hour later, still laughing about the ceiling.

"He almost fell…"

"Hey man—listen—could you do me a favor?"

"What's up?"

"I'm sick man. I'm sick. I think I must have eaten something, or—I don't know. I'm covered in spots."

"Damn."

"Yeah. Could you go to the store for me? I'll pay you back…"

"Yeah, sure. What do need, exactly?"

Tim leaves the supplies on the porch. James is still gone. Stephen and my car are still missing.

I imagine the house sounding something like the Grand Canyon, or the moon, or a graveyard.

With a little effort, I manage to crawl to the computer and look up chicken pox, small pox, poison oak, the black plague, AIDS, cancer—

The closest I can figure is I had an allergic

reaction, and to give the spots a week to clear up. I crawl back into bed.

The next day, the spots have doubled. The next day they're no better.

I've been watching Comedy Central and shivering for three days now. My stomach, sides, and legs are covered in dried calamine lotion, and I'm almost out of oranges and chicken soup.

I still haven't seen anyone, doctor, friend, clergy, drug dealer, or postman. The spots make everything blurry. And they itch and I can't scratch. They feel like millions of grains of sand, or thousands of mosquito bites.

I keep turning over. I keep crawling to the bathroom to check my face, arms, and crotch. Nothing there, at least.

Nothing to do but shiver.

The kitchen sink is roped off. The kitchen table is covered with half-eaten bowls of soup and silverware, old beer bottles, used hand towels, plates, pots, kettles, pans, pizza crusts and flies.

Dana Carvey is George H. W. Bush. Mike Myers is Dieter. Kurt Cobain is wagging his guitar and screaming through the streams of thick maroon hair that hang about his face.

At three o'clock everyday they play another movie staring Damon Wayans or Richard Pryor or Bill Murray that I've never seen. I wonder where I was when all these movies came out. I was alive then. We had a television when I was a kid. I watched The Andy Griffith Show, My Three Sons, and Bugs Bunny.

I grew up watching reruns. I grew up thinking the Beatles were still the best band in the world and

Kennedy is still president.

I remember being twelve and having my father tell me over the phone that there was a war going on in Kuwait. I had no idea. We had only just gotten to World War Two in history class.

I remember wondering when all this started. I was just about to become a teenager and there I was already questioning whether or not I had the courage to go to war if I was drafted, or if I'd hide out in Canada with all the democrats. Did I even know what democrats where then? I think my father told me they were evil.

I think the spots are fading. I've convinced myself that a week is a good number. I'll go to the doctor after a week if I'm not better and find out that I'm dying. That sounds like a good idea.

At six, I'll watch reruns of The Simpsons.

Now I'm caught up in my own mortality, and life, and all the Maxwell house commercials I'll never get to reenact.

I'd like to say I used to be a joyful child and pine away about swing sets and licorice afternoons where tiny women wore short skirts and the boys played baseball until their mothers called them in for supper on gentle dusty summer evenings. The truth is, I did play baseball. And I did pretty well in the backyard and on the playground, despite the fact that there were usually no more than four of us. But once they got us between those fences and put uniforms on us and sold hot dogs to bleachers full of heaving fathers and gossipy mothers, all my talent evaporated into my uneasy stomach. Granted, I'd get hit once a game, and usually managed to steal a base or two. But that was a gift. I swung with my eyes closed. I fielded with my eyes closed. I had the reaction time of a snowflake.

And to this day I can't remember seeing a single girl in our entire neighborhood

But we were all mad little Tom Sawyers back then. We'd skip through half-chopped forests with old abandoned woodforts and dirt fields, losing ourselves in our heads. We had tribes and villages and castles and long battles between or against pairs of brothers with full blood hits and stones and spears. We were godchildren and we were vampires.

Sometimes Brian and Jonesy and I would skip school and hit that massive field that lay behind the old church. It seemed like it was always starting to rain, and the noon blackness that came with the weather invariably corrupted our imagination. Jonesy would turn his back, we'd move in on him in dramatic slow-motion stomps, panting, pointing dead fingers and grinning evilly as our eyes grew cold. Brian would pull a pair of plastic fangs from his pocket and leap at his little brother, soon bawling and white and petrified. I'd creep up behind him chanting something from a movie I wasn't supposed to see.

Jonesy would get loose and find a crevice in the sand to hide in until our stomping got too close. In our heads imagined massive organ sounds from ancient churches and black and white monster movies.

After a few minutes, the gig was up, and Brian would goof and I'd start laughing until I had to hold my sides. Then he'd spit his teeth out, fall over and double up into the sand.

Soon we were running back at full speed, digging up dust and playing tag all the way home. Sometimes we'd see little redheaded Leonard, gang up on him, and then run before his big brothers could catch up with us.

But really, I was an ordinary child. I could have evaporated in my own dear mother's meatloaf and not many would have noticed. I was intelligent, but never brilliant. I was chubby, but never fat, funny, but never hysterical, flirtatious, but never successful.

Eventually, I grew tall enough to be thin. And all the women in high school were jealous of my eyelashes. And everyone listened when I read poetry. But in the hallway, the parking lot, the mall, the party, the fair, I was a flag, a hotdog stand, a snowflake among the storm.

Here I am, covered in spots and I never even got to play Carnegie Hall. I never asked the pretty girl to dance, and I'm pretty sure I left the oven on.

A few days later, the delirium stops, and most of the spots have vanished. My mother calls a doctor on the fifth day. She phones in a prescription without seeing me, and diagnoses my symptoms as scarlet fever.

Whatever. It doesn't matter. I'm alive. The L-shape is still there. I feel free, happy and light.

chapter three:

The Weekend Odyssey.

I.

I remember the first time I woke up anywhere. I remember the color of the ceiling, and how high. I remember thinking how bright and huge the treetops looked, and how long the sky stretched. I remember how everything felt as if nature had suddenly learned a million new colors and shapes.

I remember trying to speak with this new tongue. I remember trying to tell everyone what the sun really looked like, how music really sounded, and what art, what high ceilings, what madness, what intoxication could be had, seen, tasted, and felt. I remember the avalanche that ensued. I remember the laughter and the denial, as if I'd grown another arm rather than seen another set of ideas. I remember looking at the world again the next morning. I remember waking up in the middle of the woods, alone. I remember having to dig myself out of the ground. I remember having to make a rift where there was none.

Years pass, and I'm still in Alton. We have fourteen boat ramps, sixteen hotels, twenty shopping centers, and over sixty restaurants. I've been to every one of them.

I shave, and call Eve.

II.

I feel free, happy and light.

Eve is my oldest soldier. That alone makes it all worthwhile. But if you add to that the face for dreaming, add the pale precision and the bluest eyes, add the art in her, add the talent and the sweetness, stir it all in together and you have the girl.

III.

Before us is an open length of road. It's good to tear down the walls every now and then.

It's two hours to Washington. I wonder about all the ineluctable paths we pass on the highway. To the left is a dusty bookstore. I wonder what secrets are kept high on those shelves. Here's a little dirt road that forks a field. I wonder what adventures I'm missing. There are a thousand trees reaching airy fingers outward. I wonder what I could've taken root in. I wonder what I've neglected to plant, reap, or sow. I wonder what blossoms bloom at the end of whose fingers.

I look to the driver at my left. I remember the first time I spoke to her. She stood out even through the forests of friends. I remember the night I found her on the kitchen floor at Judy's house, sulking and beautiful. I remember how her pretty head hung.

I walked over, shaking a little, and sat down next to her as if she was a wounded animal. We started talking and the clock spun, and I told her all my underformulated ideas about man and existence. I told her how people behaved, and why, and that it wasn't her fault. I told her everyone sits on the floor sometimes. I made many puns that night that are unforgivable.

A week later, I found myself hovering over her. We were alone in a friend's room, lost in the dark without any real idea of how to hover. I remember how her touch had all the numbing anger of vodka, all of the sickness, the light head, and diffused eyes. I remember it had all of that, and none of the hangover. We spent a month like that.

I remember the color of the carpet where I sat with my head in her lap while she ran her fingers through my hair.

One day it all just dissolved. The ocean I'd been swimming in became the foam on the beach, and the water left to pursue a new shoreline. I just stood there staring into the bleaching, blinding sun, not knowing how or why the world revolved.

It took me years to get over the ocean.

IV.

Happy and light.

After Eve, I left Alton for a few years and went west. I got a job and a girl, and she was every pretty girl on every front porch in every suburb. And her name was Lola Thomas.

I guess I imaged that was belonging. I guess I imagined, because the job was steady and the pay was decent. I guess I imagined because her body fit, and her eyes flickered.

One day I just quit my job. I don't know if it was out of boredom or because of an argument, or what. I just quit. And I—I didn't have the heart to find another one. I hated living there. I'd spent all my time with Lola. I couldn't find a goddamned grocery store without her. I couldn't stand my own mind.

It's hard now to say where I was—and what was waste—and what was wonder.

There are fourteen boat ramps, sixteen hotels, twenty shopping centers, and over sixty restaurants. I find that both comforting and utterly horrifying. Lola followed me here. I still don't know why. Right now I can't even tell if I care. Sometimes I think I just fell in loved with her record collection.

Time is nothing now. There are no appointments and no alarms. There are no papers or additions due. There are no L-shapes, or off tempo heartbeats. Before us is an open length of road. Before us are endless islands and the sea.

V.

Just outside the city Eve trades me the wheel. Buildings bloom around us like wildflowers. Cars chase the grey pollen of cars.

Eve can't drive in the city because she isn't made of stone or steel. Eve would do better planted in a garden in the sun.

I feel like I've been gone from her for so long. For the last two years I've only seen her in the occasional dream, or spoken to her briefly across a wire. Now she's sitting next to me, smiling politely.

When she's happy, her eyes bend down into the curve of her smile. When she's uncomfortable, her brow betrays her, and slants off the other way, and her front teeth seem slightly more crooked than usual.

Sometimes, this color of kindness worries me. She smiles so much, that the natural intoxicant of her mood infects everyone. And she can't help but continue.

No one ever told her that compassion can kill if aimed just off center. Just as the narcotic cannot choose its beneficiary, Eve cannot choose the recipient of her smile. It pervades everything. And like the drug, the more you use it, the more you want it, and the less you'll feel her. And the more placid and glassy your skin becomes, and the more hers becomes misused.

This is one reason it's wrong to run into Eve. Sometimes you wonder if you are running into her arms, into her empathy, or into some kind of western mirage. It's so soft there, so sincere, so numb. But it might all just be sand.

I remember lying with my head in her lap. I remember looking straight up. I can still see the color of the ceiling.

Cars crowd all sides. The right lane is ephemeral. Streets exchange lanes for parking spots for lanes.

We drive soberly past the archaic fences that act as spinal columns for daisies. New York Avenue spills into small circles of highway. New states are born on each turn.

VI.

To the right, row houses hang sarcastic signs. The sound of a television pours through an open window. The smell of streaking feet on concrete combines with car exhaust and old brick sweat to fill the air. We are here.

We enter deftly, and then circle the street for the subway.

The escalator at the entrance drops six stories straight down. And everyone is falling so casually.

I don't dare look down. I hate heights. I want to grab Eve right there and close my eyes so tight.

At the bottom a thousand little worker bees move back and forth on a line. They all look so similar—as if God has run out of extras.

Overhead, a literal concrete honeycomb stretches as far as the eye can see. Something groans from far off in the distance. I wonder if bees ever feel like they're being digested.

We're well into the concave concrete belly of the city. I can see its spine arching above. Its stomach is pale and empty.

Eve and I hop gates and march through giant sets of grated teeth. Giant metal caterpillars chase each other down concrete cavities, making awful moans that could only have been manufactured by a man.

We board one of the monsters, and I watch the bubbling hieroglyphics spin by through the windows. Eve smiles and flutters her eyelashes.

Despite my best efforts I still get a little flutter sitting next to her.

VII.

Out on the street, Eve grins like a child in space. There's something different in every direction. She hops, pauses, skips, spins and falls without knowing which way to go first.

Little galleries line Connecticut Avenue. We find one that's filled with an endless array of tiny clay ducks. Some displays seat hundreds of personified waterfowl standing in a single clay bowl. Others exhibit single figures lying in bathtubs painted like Jackson Pollock or Vincent Van Gogh. The man at the door disappears and Eve and I laugh violently. A thousand clay ducks. Someone took the time to create a thousand fucking clay ducks.

Down the street, a kind old German invites us in his own gallery. The first floor is filled with square abstracts resembling geometric puffins. From now on I will always associate the city with waterfowl.

Upstairs, we wander through a collection of paintings, sketches and sculptures. The old German asks if we are artists. Eve replies—

"I'm an art major."

To which the old German is quiet. He seems

thoughtfully disappointed, and tells us to return in spring.

It's cold out on the streets. The wind blows us in every direction. Long aisles of pavement are parted by grass and sand. Circling city buildings look like so many mountains.

Soon, we're wandering through a sculpture garden. Eve seeks out the more familiar pieces of steel and stone and calls out everything:

"Matisse, Picasso, some damned Greek…"

Ceci n'est pas une pipe!

I watch the aimless endeavors of children, dancing around such odd old stone. They hop walls like knights in imaginary castles, not knowing that what they're dancing around may have been made before castles. They're at that point in childhood where laughter is the only language. Before words. Before fingerprints. They're at that point when memory is still a thing to be pulled from the air.

Inside the bigger galleries, we witness that fine intellectual balance between beauty and garbage. I think talent must be as frequent as sand in the desert, but sometimes I think it's as important as affection in the middle of an ocean.

We take turns laughing and dropping our jaws. This thin red line on a white canvas does not impress me. That bronzed three-dimensional photograph of the city does.

This poor soul lamenting his lover in bizarre charcoal cartoons amazes us both. I'm sure I'm an old Russian at heart. I love the dreary cold romanticism. It's all carbon and communism. It's all so bleak. I'm frozen in its nothingness. I'm sitting underground remembering my youth. There's a hammer in my heart. There's a black hole in my refrigerator.

I am black and white sketches of Russian factory workers. I am small eyes poised against the infinite sickle. I adore the sensitivity of death, and nothingness. I've always believed that the cold can only make you appreciate the sweetness so much more.

VIII.

Outside, we ford the streets like rivers. You have to hop and paddle and dive and forgive the wave if it catches and carries you away.

Along the banks and away from the art we are to remember what the city is here for—that what is populated is productive.

Shops in gold-trimmed, but faded glass show off a pastry here, a dress there, an office, a film, the future. This place has been here for ages and always will. That space is just as ephemeral as our pockets allow.

There's a hunger in us now. Hunger is deeply and Evenly divided between the head, the heart, and the stomach. I will feed the only one I can.

Off the gallery block is a small Spanish restaurant with a clear glass front. The walls inside are covered in early twentieth century abstract art done in heavy yellows, browns and blacks. We sit down and order glasses of port and I immediately feel like Ernest Hemingway.

Eve eats constant salads. She nibbles at food and love as if they were tied together. She's afraid that either one will, with weight, conspire against movement.

And I'm sure she's right, but I am disappointed regardless.

Small talk among old friends and artists are always about ideas rather than events. We haven't had a bad day's work or concerns over late bills. Rather, we are picturing the future with the proper disregard of the dreamer.

I can tell she's picturing my thoughts. I can tell she knows the questions and that I'll avoid the answers. She twirls an oil-soaked forkful of lettuce. I order a scotch.

"So Charlie—where would you like to be right now—if you could be anywhere?"

I look her in the eye and pause as if to say, "you know where I want to be."

I would be in the middle of the ocean looking at the outline of your face as the sun sinks and steals light. I would memorize every line before the light disappeared. I would lie awake all night drawing the outline. And in the morning, I would drown.

I know I can't be honest. So I'll be the next best thing. I'll be *pretentious.*

"I would be in Paris, writing. I would feast on the Notre Dame, sitting with my back against the white stone walls just off the Seine. I would wander the Louvre, Moderne, and Picasso. I would walk boastfully by the rude Frenchmen in the shops surrounding Montparnasse smoking American cigarettes. I would spend all day in the theaters watching American films with French subtitles.

And I wouldn't learn a word of French. I would become so completely devoid of conversation— I would become so alien to speaking—that for fear of atrophy I would be forced to write over a hundred novels a year. I would sit around all day having imaginary conversations with stones and little grey finches named Gavroche. I would invent a dream language apart from anything anyone has ever seen or heard.

And then I'd go to Père Lachaise and dig up Jim Morrison. I'd restore his skin and stuff his body with sawdust. I'd reunite him with Arthur Rimbaud and see them married at Versailles. They'd come to life and burn the whole damned palace down.

And then I'll have Lennon restored. I'll have someone fill him up with air so I could parade around the beaches with my balloon poet for world peace. I would become a serious artist. I'd start painting the dead with the living. I'd aim to create confusion and paradox before substance."

Eve, who began cringing, is now laughing at the ridiculousness of the dream and the heavy hand gestures that aid in the absurdity.

"Et toi, mon ami?"

"Hmmm…I always wanted to go to Africa and take pictures of wildlife. Lions, and rhinoceroses, and toucans, and tigers. Oh! And Madagascar! I'd be on an island in another world, taking pictures of all the images I could never find here. Maybe I'd move in with a tribe of handicapped cannibals and earn awards for photographic research."

"And then you'd be eaten."

"And then you'd fill what's left with air and fly me around Venice like a kite."

"I think you've had enough port…"

"You're right," holding up her glass and giggling, "Garçon? Can I get this to go?"

IX.

The crowds are thick outside. The cold makes everyone seem hurried and unfriendly.

Eve and I duck into a corner to catch a smoke. An old woman walks by giving us evil looks. We watch her round the corner and burst out laughing.

It's strange smoking cigarettes in the winter. You can't tell the difference between the smoke and steam coming out of your throat. It's strange to be at once cold and on fire.

Off urbane comforts, we head back towards the guttural underworld of mass transit. If the streets are rapids, then the subway stairs are the foreboding waterfalls just over the rocks.

Looking down, it seems like miles. It's funny to watch everyone slide down so easily. I wonder if they know they're going over the edge. I wonder if they'd catch me if I jumped.

At the bottom you can look up and see the bones lining the belly that swallowed you. We board an artery and watch the graffiti lining spinning by and I convince myself that it's okay to mix metaphors in the city.

Outside, a black woman yells at an old building that used to be a Burger King. We ask her for directions; she signals left, and then resumes shouting at imaginary fast food restaurants.

X.

The bridge into Georgetown is high and narrow. We are nearly cornered by the cars that honk and wheeze at our sides. But they quickly become confused and useless at seeing our legs moving faster than their wheels.

The sidewalks are one long marketplace that slope downward with the setting sun.

The images here are far from presbytery. Little idiosyncratic shops blink neon lights from glass windows. Inside each are odd post-modern store clerks pretending to be bored and sophisticated. One window displays clothing that looks like modified plastic shower curtains. Another exhibits what looks to be furniture from futuristic cartoons.

XI.

There's an enormous bookstore across the street. The second story has a café with thin wooden tables painted olive-green, and a row of booths in the back.

"Come on, I'll buy you a cup of coffee—"

Eve shivers and nods happily.

Inside we arm ourselves with music magazines and sink into the olive booths with styrofoams of steaming coffee. Eve doesn't notice as I zone off into the exposed slope of her neck that winds down into her shoulders going bronze to gold. Her skin is whiter than the cream in her coffee. We must look like vampires with heroin habits.

Sometimes I forget how good she looks. Sometimes her skin sings to remind me.

I don't say a word.

XII.

Eve isn't a lamb. But I made her seem like one. Lola isn't a monster. But I made her.

I used to fall for kindness. I've had a gear or too drawn into my eye by kindness. But no more. I pulled the wool over my eyes, and I snuck out on Eve's belly.

After a while, you get tired of saving people.

I'm too young to always be the cradle. I'm too young to always be the water and never the wave. You were ash on my eyes. You were the smoke in my mirror. But no more.

Goodbye.   Goodbye.

I left like a deserter from war. I walked off and left you
on the battlefield. I heard you screaming as I grew distant. I
pulled the wool over my eyes, and I snuck out on Eve's belly.
I lost ten years staring at the slope of her neck.

XIII.

We came here oddly enough. I woke up
running, and ended up in museums and under
waterfalls. In-between I talked to the natives. I even
looked one or two of them in the eye.

Now we've washed up in Georgetown and
become enamored with store windows and commercial
coffee.

We came here oddly enough. I woke up feeling
lost, and by dusk I am already reverting back to the
same old daydreams.

Now the only thing to do is to find our way
back.

Cars rumble slowly underground, coughing out
commuters. We walk down white stone stairs, and up
jagged metal teeth that bend heavenward forever.

We end on shady concrete. The sun has set,
leaving only the pale glow of city light.

The evening begins to fold the world in its
mysterious embrace. Eve and I begin the search for
landmarks in earnest. Find the North Star. Find the
theater. Find the intersection of Florida and T.

XIV.

But even the familiar is unfamiliar in the dark.

We head down Florida past S street. What
looked like kind Victorian pillars during the day are now
dreary curmudgeons. The pale smoke born in

manholes has become the slow, portentous hiss of the slums.

"Not that way…that's not the way Charlie. It didn't look like that...it couldn't have…"

We walk into a convenience store. Its patrons and clerks seem unnaturally astonished. We must look like vampires.

Eve asks about the theater. It's the only thing we can remember from the day.

"Ain't no movie theater 'round here. Hey! Jamie! You know anything about a movie place?"

"Ain't nothing like that around here…"

"I don't know. You best be careful though. Good luck…"

There isn't a streetlight for miles.

Eve becomes tense, and I can hear her mumbling,

"Dear Lord—deliver us in safety…"

We are here. I can see by the unmended canyons in the road. I can see by the dusty deserted shop windows. We are here.

I always thought I knew what it was like. I always thought it was enough out of the wombfruit to know about being lost, or being confused, or feeling out of place. I always thought that that would translate. But there's no language here. What good are words when you have no voice?

I stare straight, inventing knives in my eyes.

What good is language when everything looks the same? It's as if poverty invented space. It's as if the forests of buildings we saw earlier were replaced by beaches of glass. Here, the hum of the ocean is replaced by the drone of the dead.

It's as if poverty invented abandonment. Or maybe money invented rejection. I don't know. Either way, I'm in the middle of it.

Back home, the slums mean an occasional crack pipe that washes up on the sidewalk, or a couple of kids walking the streets past midnight.

Here it's all a pretty dream. Those figures in that alley aren't real. They can't see us. They're not walking this way.

Evil is always thickest in movies. Nothing can. Nothing can. Nothing can harm.

Everything is too personified. We're walking too fast. Part of me wants to stop and pinch the ground. Part of me wants to stop and ask questions. Most of me wants to run.

Nothing is real. Nothing is valid anymore. We are in the middle of the ocean staring at four corners of fins. The only question is whose teeth first.

I corner myself against the current, hide Eve and hope whatever beast born is full quickly.

Remember the meaning of the day. Remember who mends and who heals. Remember what it felt like in the air. You're going there now Charlie.
Look forward. All sides now. Cast no shadow.

Eve clutches my side and whispers once more for safety.

"Our father who art…bless us…deliver us…"

Daggers and eyes. My frail frame and her slender womanhood. We're like two pretty twigs and I expect to frighten armies with my eyes.

Look forward.

This street is less perilous than that one. We walk toward what could be a theater, but the theater is a mirage.

We're out of ideas.

XV.

From the dimness of the uncobbled streets emerge two stealthy skeletons. Their posture is bent forward like an open mouth. Their voices are the hissing drone of the dead. We are here.

The one on the left curses under his breath in step—

"Mutha fuckas!"

step—

"Gowin down!"

step—

"Wrong goddamn place…"

step—

"Wrong—god—damn—time."

step—

Now they're inches behind us. I can feel their breath beating down on the back of my neck. I imagine a bullet or a blade ready. I imagine the last sensations I ever will.

Remember those dreams, remember the feeling of falling? Remember when you woke and it was only the floor? This isn't the floor, Charlie.

Remember everything you wrote as a child. Remember wishing for silence.

step—

Something grabs onto my arm. I hold my breath.

Eve pulls me sharply to the right. The door opens and the light inside is positively blinding.

We're inside a hospital. There's a hospital in the

middle of the ocean. Our shadows walk by, unphased.
Gasp and pause. Safe. Happy and light.

XVI.

A loud-lipped receptionist interrogates us. We
tell her we think we are lost.

"Florida and T? Well that should be right down
the block but—I don't know about no movie theater.
What's it called?"

Eve describes the surroundings down to the
angle of the cracks in the road.

"There's a movie theater…and little
galleries…Victorian houses…ivy vines …a sign on the
door that said…"

"Don't forget the ducks…"

A large, well-featured black man in a white
overcoat overhears us.

"That sounds like Connecticut Ave. I think
Florida and T cross around there as well."

"How far is it?"

"Ha! Are you trying to walk or drive?" He
pulls us aside. "You know, I wouldn't walk around in
this neighborhood at this time of night. It's not too
safe. Look—why don't you call a cab? There's a phone
on the desk over there…"

Eve blesses him. Her eyes twitch emphatically.
"Thank you so much!"

He laughs. "Sure thing. Buck up now. Be
safe…"

Write this on the wall. It's mystery that man
fears best. It's poverty rather than skin. We give names
to the sun and moon just as we apply evil to the
darkness. But it's mystery that man fears.

Whoever hears whispers is appreciated.

XVII.

A cab drops us across the street from my car. In front of us are three black men. The man in the middle is dressed like a minister. Whoever hears whispers is appreciated.

At the door, I pull Eve into the air and spin her around, like in the endings of all old movies.

Inside the car we recline seats and split a cigarette. I could burst I could burst I could burst.

We move the car a few streets down to the Black Cat.

Inside, a girl with jagged blonde hair and combat boots throws a guitar into its case and jumps off stage. Eve and I have a seat on the floor and wait.

A few cigarettes later, a middle aged, overweight white man wearing a long silk robe climbs over us and onto the stage. He pushes the play button on a silver box and starts to sing—

"Don't you even bother to knock

"Cause you might throw off my rock—"

And then the overweight middle aged bald white throws off his robe to reveal a ridiculously poor rendition of an Elvis costume. He falls back on one hand, and thrusts his hips up at the audience.

By the end of the first song the crowd is near tears in laughter.

"What's my name?"

"Harmar Superstar!"

"What's my name?"

"Harmar Superstar!"

"Buy my record!"

By the third song he's already sold you his soul, eaten a bowl of Cocoa Puffs and borrowed his brother's van to go to a keg party with your daughter. His expression is so convincingly and unflinchingly stoical.

Between sets, something looking like an extra from Animal House walks over to Eve.

"Hey! You're so pretty! What the hell are you doing here? You're beautiful!"

I step in, aware of the beer glasses in each hand. "Hi…"

"Hey man, great to see you. How've you been? Wonderful! Why don't you walk the fuck over there?"

The next act looks like Drew Carey gone convincingly punk rock. He plays guitar over the same silver box that backed-up Harmar.

Meanwhile, a shorthaired woman in a bad leather jumpsuit leans into Eve. I'm now officially the only person on the planet who hasn't made a pass at her.

A few minutes later, the frat boy stammers back, bearing more bottles now than ever. He throws one arm around a guy with a green mohawk and the other around what appears to be David Bowie's bastard son.

Halfway through the set, he falls over, simultaneously knocking down a section of the crowd and unplugging the stage sound. He finally lands sharply on Eve's ankle, and lies there for a minute looking rather peaceful. Assholes are invincible.

Outside the wooden womb of the Cat, we steal great breaths of stale city air. Today, we stood in the cold and shivered. Today we grew shadows in the ghetto, guarded against drunks, defeated bridges, and upped escalators. Today, I had my eyes open. Today I never felt like running from myself.

Today I realized:

I'd follow her through the fire
just to see
what happens.

XVIII.

It's two hours back. We stop a few times for food, or air, or sleeping drivers. Breakfast in bitch, coffee behind the wheel.

We pass the dusty bookstores, dirt roads and the thousand trees that reach airy fingers and bloom.

And she holds me in the driveway. Briefly. And she speeds away as the eyes of the world grow smaller.

chapter four:

Le Sommeil se Prolonge

Eve Saul stares at a pile of glasses laid on a table. A bit of fabric is curled behind for the background, and the wood grain foreground, barren save for a few toppled, empty wineglasses, is lacking something like a human touch. I sit behind her on the floor amazed at the lifeless thing she is recreating on canvas.

"Why don't you throw in an ashtray and a half lit cigarette off to the side in that left corner?"

She stops moving for a second and listens.

"And a maybe a little smoke—right there. Add a little bit of—life inside the stillness."

"Hmm…" She sweeps her brush in the air and nods her head as her bottom lip curls into a smile. "Perfect!" Her left eyebrow reaches up unevenly, as if to suggest something wicked.

I'm sitting uncomfortably close to the future.

An hour ago, sitting in the car she said, "I feel strange—funny."

"Good funny or bad funny?"

"Good—just—sort of—out of it. Strange."

And then she blinked and looked away as if she'd accidentally let something loose that she shouldn't have.

Does this mean you feel it too, Eve? I imagine you must in moments like these. I imagine gravity affects all life forms.

If there's a tension between us, it's the tension of sea against air. If you feel something, it's the tension of smooth strokes and silence. It's the tension of great waves against a rocky cliff, of retracting and changing currents, or foam and rain, gentle and solemn, or of bubbling eventuality.

O N E

Quixotic Nod.

Haze. Haze. Haze. Lead me through all my days. I wake up in a liquid state. Some days I feel like I could swim better than I could walk.

I lie there in that morning womb, wondering. My body feels stiff and unreliable. My eyes strain to see even the fog. My head is weighted, but feels no burden buried there.

Imagine living in this fog forever. Imagine rolling around, constant, in the uninjuring morning— laughing to imagine the man outside on the sidewalk marching with his briefcase and brown hat. All day he moves mechanically to the tune of his own personal pied piper, productivity.

Or see the mothering ruin her pretty hair, pulling once each day for each screaming child she cannot calm. Eventually even the dullness of her veins becomes more pronounced. She sings to it, "talk damnit! Tell me how! What! I'm listening! Wake!" As it only blinks and is startled.

The child is hardly ever as bothered by things as the mother.

Then imagine never having to bare the borders of living, or if this is at all possible. Eve always liked to stay out of situations that could become difficult. Now she tells me she's afraid of the repercussions of friendship in the past tense, as if anything great and lasting falls onto your doorstep magically.

The world isn't easy, Eve. One day we'll all be

briefcasing to the confused choruses of children. But to battle now is to understand the time, for this is the mechanism for war. To battle is to have an interest in the outcome. To battle is to desire to be free.

Something sounds like an alarm, but I'm not worried.

The Arms of Morpheus.

It all seems so ordinary in the dark.

Eve comes over at night. We walk across the street to the grocery store for florescent light bulbs and microwaveable Italian dinners.

We have a drink... food...

Watch something on television that will never matter...

And then she just rolls over and falls asleep. I turn the lights out and the television off. And I curl close but not too close as to be around.

And I shiver like I haven't in years.

And there's movement there, I can almost see the outline of an unfamiliar road. It looks like new pavement stamped over an empty, stretching space.

And no horizon means no end. The only thing in the distance is the colored bending of light and sky.

A little strip of her stomach is exposed. It bends in and curves outwards unto her hips. It's smooth and seamless. Like water.

She breathes in an exaggeration of air, slow and heavy, even laborious. She breathes in deeply and then swiftly out through her mouth. Then she grows quiet, as if she was storing air so she might eventually stop breathing altogether.   Now she is motionless, sound and seemingly comfortable. I've finally made enough comfort to create this. My existence is finally merit enough for marvel.

And what rare flashes of the future flicker now,

like hopeful lightening. A little pocket of her face hangs below a line of blue pillows facing me. Her lips point straight up at the ends and part slightly at the middle as if she is about to blow a kiss. I am paralyzed with joy.

Sometime into the night, she turns on her side. And, as if to quiet some lingering voice in my head, I roll over and curl around her. My arms run through hers as her back arches into the angle of my chest. And I can see her whole face now. There's not an arc of a smile, but there's something even more peaceful, like the last shiver before a fire. I could call it classical, timeless, ageless, endless, faceless, shapeless, soundless, scentless, or ghost-like. I could compare it to something rising in the east, or a blooming from the ground, or to the way New York must look to an American who is seeing for it the first time.

I drive her home in the morning.

She coughs and I pull over at a gas station to buy her cough drops. If she shivered, I'd buy her a blanket. If she was hungry, I'd buy her a grocery store. If she was lonesome, I'd buy her a small Caribbean Island and populate it. We head back down the long and desolate early Sunday morning road.

Chimera.

And then she disappears for a few days.

And then she just walks back into my life as if time were a thing like blinking. She's wearing a red cotton shirt that hangs down well below the neck, revealing all God built to defy gravity.

And I'm well-past drunk when she arrives. And I'll be drunker still when she leaves. I know the newborn buzz and bloom that love opens up in your liver, and that eventually settles like a rock into your stomach.

Red cotton hangs low off her neck, looking no thicker than the morning mist on spring grass. I just lay there and watch the world as it opens up and starts to spin, like sped-up footage of a flower blooming.

Her legs bend into triangles around my brain. Her voice hangs like a whisper in an empty tin room.

Morphine and Morphia.

The lines of her face are to rivers feeding fields. And from those lines, a radiant grey light grows that is the essential and worldly sadness that ultimately becomes the shape for goodness, or that pronounces "wonder." I imagine that everything inside her is just as luminous as the perfect, peaceful image of her face.

Each time I wake in the night, I find myself still deeply involved in the crescent moon curves of woman.

The alarm rings out angrily, but I destroy the sound and sink slowly backwards. An hour later, when we rise for good, I am willing to remove my arms around her, but I am unwilling to remove the shine.

Somnolent.

The scent of love is like the scent of death sometimes. Each strikes you the same. Each takes the wind out of your lungs. Each over-pronounces your eyes.

She lived, and what now? I loved and now there is this—silence. Its ring hangs just between death and eternity.

Somnoritic.

The ringing. I answer the phone. The voice at the other end is calm, careful not to pronounce any inflections of change. I'd like to tell it to go away, but instead I ask it to dinner.

Some time later, there is a little echo. There are the usual glances and welcoming words. There is that irrational voice that is the sea.

I look up gingerly. My eyes glow of hollow automatic affection. My head tilts in the direction of hope. Somehow.

Somnific.

I look down, and ask her with all the confidence of a mortician:

"Look—is there anything I shouldn't get the wrong idea about? I mean—I can never really tell with you. And I—I can't ever seem to jump when it's this…meaningful. I can't find the courage. If I'm going to fall, I'll have to be pushed…"

She smiles warmly and ghost-like, and stirs her drink. She stirs ten years as if it really were just gin. She holds the straw between her fingers as if it weren't beating. She rattles the ice as if it actually enjoyed being shaken.

Somnifacient.

My eyelids flap like the excited wings of a butterfly. I look out the window. Leaves burn and fall and receive snow. The sun rises and sets. People streak by on comedic feet. Leaves fall and receive snow and dissolve. The sun rises and sets. Buildings are erected in a blur. Leaves receive snow and dissolve and become food. The sun rises and sets like elapsed-time footage from science class. Leaves dissolve and become the food feeding spring. Like elapsed-time footage.

Somniferous.

Then something red and saucer-shaped blooms. And her hand holds back an intrusive streak of her hair. And she leans forward, eyes ahead. Her eyes open, so wide, so blue, and then shut so tight.

Nepenthean.

I'd yawn if I could move.

An old movie plays on the television atop the dresser. Our eyes claim to focus on it, but our bodies twist together and then apart like two teasing tides.

She rolls on her back and shifts her legs against mine, folding them so neatly together, and then so far apart.

Her legs aren't as clever as her hands. Leaves fall. People walk by on comedic feet.

Eve carves her head a home in my shoulder, and at once I feel myself waking and regressing into sleep.

My heart beats a drum roll into my chest and then relaxes and then dies. My fingers find the line of hair that leads into her neck and extends to the back of her head.

Maybe there'll be no more discomfort or disillusion after this. Maybe she's settled now. Maybe in the morning there'll be love tangles and bad breath kisses. Maybe there'll be cracked-lip smiles and sore arms wound around warm bodies. Maybe I'll tell her about balconies and poets, about ivy stairs and the wings on idealism. Maybe I'll tell her it's gold in here.

A mirror! Armor! Amor!

I know I flew here last night somehow. I know
I spent something with someone.

Eve arrives late looking hollow and over-pale.
She stumbles in and pleads a drink.

"…have had the worst day…"

And I take her in my arms. And it's something
between a battered child and an adoring father. Either
way, I will hold her through it. Either way she will
always be in my head, past the point of disagreement
and stuck somewhere between family and
unconditional.

Her body feels good against mine. She holds on
tighter knowing I would never injure her the way the
rest of the world would. I have stood the storm through
and am now eyeing the rainbow in baggy jeans and a
black tank top.

> *"all here is clear now*
> *look forward, angel…"*

When she drives away I am left feeling confused
and lucky.

Recognition.

Something rings and I wake up. "Hello?"

TWO

Mémoires d'outre-tombe.

Adam was *her* first love. Adam had a cleft jaw
and job offers in government intelligence.

Adam lived hundreds of miles away. Adam took

advantage.

Adam was her religious match. He met her at a ministry meeting in Tennessee. He took to her beauty and she took to his. No one seemed to notice that he was a mathematician and she was a painter.

They fell in love, divided distance, and then gradually disappeared. Just like that. Distance does strange things.

She still cries a little at the thought of him. She's crying now. I want to tell her she never knew him well enough to realize his weaknesses. I want to tell her he was never real enough to justify tears.

She's thinking about writing him a letter.

· · · · · · · · · ·

The radio alternates Donna Summer and Marvin Gaye. How disco and Motown ever get crossed is beyond me.

Eve, oblivious, dances badly around a large canvas of fragmented flowers. I roll around the empty classroom on a metal filing cabinet with squeaking and directionless wheels. The room is filled with pink mannequins who seem to've traded arms for eerie eyes, brows, lips, and the indentations of genitalia. Green glass jugs, seashells, pipe parts, and old brown bohemian boots surround the plastic basket cases in oddly arranged still life scenes.

The walls around us are littered with paintings, sketches, studies, sculptures, silhouettes, streaks, spaces, sparse speechless skylines, green apple allegories, bent benches blooming into backgrounds where wooden walls wait further attention, old alcoholic jugs, and dead drying discarded displays dancing on the rolling rings of wheeled wandering metal chariots.

To the left are clay bananas bent into obvious

phalluses that brashly mock the stoned sentimental harmony of colors and chalk-smoke stowed atop towering particleboard buildings.

Eve sways slowly to the dated harmony of the Jackson Five. She sings along like an angel of alphabets while her right hand keeps the beat with a hardened paintbrush.

She coughs thoughtfully, pauses to ponder the color of the sixteenth square from the top left, backs away, nods in approval at the series of cubes that have been evolving into a cloud, dips into the blue and starts the skyline.

Eve herself is wearing three shades of blue.

....

The trees stand out against the sky like cardboard cutouts on paper. The green against the grey make an odd disharmony out of dull colors, and the contradiction of streetlamps and the rain soaked road relate only to the flickering storm in the sky.

This is my first fix of the day. I live on porches smoking cigarettes for the five minutes of calm and reflection they provide. I'm best just after it starts to rain, and the sky isn't yet covered, and there's just a hint of stars.

Drops of rain accumulate on the roof and make waterfalls. I wonder how many drops of rain my roof can hold. I wonder how the rain falls and never asks why.

Tonight I've read, rained, written, and regarded. Sometimes all of this is enough. Sometimes the storm, its melodies, thoughts, backgrounds, and waterfalls are enough. Sometimes the glimmering lights, trees, bare feet, open windows, music—

The _____ of sound.

A thud rings, echoes, shakes, hangs in the air until plucked by a knowing ear. A single sound—a note by a bird, or a footstep—is nothing. But a multitude of these sounds, several notes, steps, vibrations, or tones together—that becomes a rhythm, a melody.

Melody makes my inside shiver. I could curl up forever inside a shaking voice, stuttering like a child or set against the rhythm of factory machines, or a lone trumpet singing an elegy on a Sunday afternoon in the city.

Or the joy of the choir, the accumulation, or a guitar being banged like an indignant nail, announcing its vitality by measure of sheer volume. Or the thunderclap of drums beaten because the man has vitality, the woman beauty, the child hope, the human existence—

A drum beaten because the world spins and yet we stay still. A drum beaten like a heartbeat. Racing or rest. Solid or slow and graceful. Moody or delicate.

Music is the range of man.

I pace the yard with the stub of a cigarette still hanging from my lower lip. I'm staring at the sky and at what cracks in the clouds I can make in my mind. I have this entire atmosphere. I have oxygen, carbon, nitrogen and rain. I have the swaying silhouettes of birches. I have music and all those things invented in shadows.

I wonder how many drops of rain my roof can hold. I wonder how the rain falls and never asks why.

Bonfire and the Vanity.

I am going to tell her everything. I'm going to tell her about the motionless mornings, alone. I'm going to tell her about streetlights echoing sound. I'm going to tell her about the hole in my stomach and the ringing in my ears. I'm going to tell her how the space is deafening.

I'm going to tell her how other women have become featureless, and that desire is full of ash. I'm going to tell her that fires only burn so long, and that every fire dies.

I'm going outside.

I'm going to tell her it's loud enough to be in love, and how the spinning, spaces, moods, memories, and motions are all fools for gravity. I'm going to tell her that love=love despite what walls men and women erect around their hearts.

I'm going to tell her with such conviction that no man under no balcony holding no glossary of Shakespeare, or catalogue of Cyrano could come within a hundred miles of me. I'm going to do it all with such sadness, gladness, gravity, air, ease, strain, sickness, and hope.

I'm going to open the door.

And I'll tuck that shock of hair behind her left ear. And I'll roll my fingers under her chin and down the side of her neck until she shivers. And I'll dive into her eyes the way the sun stares into a river, unbending and bright. Stark. Beautiful.

I'm going to empty everything. I'm going to empty entire that sad, strained well of waiting.

I'm going to start the car.

I'm going to let the monster loose. I'm going to take that hanging, overdue idea and build it a body. If there are villagers, there'll be torches and pyres, vigils, mobs, and ministers. I'm going to cover it with zirconium and fool's gold.

I'm going to pave over her past, for this is the rough beast between us now.

I'm going to show her how unworthy memory is of the future, and how progress is achieved. I'm going to show her how to move out of the valley and into the sky.

The car skips pebbles down empty back roads, holding tight onto turns as if not a thing made of metal.

I'm going to turn left.

I can see her house from here. I can see her in the doorway, waiting.

I'm going to show her how it can be with a poet.

She's wearing that green wool jacket that's she's had since high school. She looks hip and lean, slouching with cobalt blue eyes that would echo desolation if not for pink, pursed lips.

I exit the machine staring straight ahead, brows bent for the impending gravity, or for that moment in air between the ground and heaven and nothingness.

She knows instantly. I can tell she is braced for something. I've lost my cover already.

No matter now. I'm in the air. I'm falling. The only thing left is to convince her to open her arms.

"Eve—there's—there's something I want to say. There's something I've wanted to say for a long time."

"Charlie…"

"Just—just listen for a minute, okay? Okay. Ah, look—I've been thinking. I know—I know you're still holding onto Adam. I know you only remember the good about him—like that time he drove three hours for a kiss, or those handmade valentines he sent you that crumbled in the mail. Or that video he made of his hometown and his friends, so you wouldn't feel so far from him even across two time zones.

Or that first time you slept together after a year of tension. And how nothing ever felt like that.

You remember all of this—but you forget about the disappearing. You forget about the months after when he was silent when you needed him the most. You forget that he never had any fucking grasp of art whatsoever, and that you are an artist.

You remember all those fucking ideal things he did. You invented this image of him the way little girls make princes and dragons. You imagined this ineffable white knight without remembering the pain, or the incomplete character, or the disappearing.

You're holding onto this—and you're afraid— you're terrified that nothing new could ever live up to what he's become in your head. You're afraid to destroy the image that you created. But at the same time, you remember the pain he left you with. And you're afraid to feel something real again because you think it might disappear. And—you know I disappear. You know I disappear often.

And that's why you travel in ten different circles. And this is why you went out with Tom last summer, who you compared endlessly to me, who wasn't me. This is why you went out with that other fuck, who had none of the depth, or even the exterior. This is why you went without substance or attraction— because everything has to be so safe with you, everything has to be light. Everything has to have an out.

I know you still believe in the past. But it's all a fucking myth now! It's a story you invented to deter yourself from ever being free.

You think—you think this is what happens when you trust someone. But Eve—this—is what happens to everyone. Love wouldn't be so exhilarating if it didn't hurt so goddamned much when it's gone.

No one likes to fall. Sometimes, I'm even afraid to breathe. But I'm not going to stop. Stop one and stop all. Stop air and stop living. Stop love and stop dreaming. Stop dreaming and there's nothing left. Air is meaningless to a broken heart. I know.

And God—you still make me shiver. To this day.

Sometimes I think you're the same shade of the past for me that Adam is for you. And I shiver, because for all the beauty, for all the art, for all the time, for everything you know about me and care for me, there is still this layer of ice around you. And you built that. And only you can climb out. I've used every match and fire I could, I've used everything. Only you can climb out now.

I'm afraid too, goddamnit. I know how long we've known each other, and I know how much danger there is in crossing that line. But the tension is there. The tension has been there, and will be there. There are no roads behind us. We're no more two innocent kids playing in the sand. And none of this would be worthwhile without the fear. There wouldn't be any weight without the fear.

And nothing worthwhile is ever easy. And nothing easy is ever lasting. There's only to hope and try. The world's full of death and disappointment. If it weren't for the possibility of peaks—I wouldn't have lasted this long. I probably would have followed Blake a long time ago...when he...

Sometimes I think he did the right thing...you..."

Eve is quiet. I can tell she feels cornered. I can tell I did it all wrong. She pauses for a second and I breathe.

"But none of this matters, does it? I really couldn't say anything to you. None of this matters."

I turn toward the car, and I can hear her saying:

"Charlie—Charlie wait!" behind me.

And now I speak softer. "God—you act so fucking innocent all the time. You act as if you've never done anything wrong, as if we're all to blame for falling in love with you. Well, fuck you Eve. Fuck you. If nothing else, you've committed into my brain the repeat offense of hope."

And she pauses like a river after the echoes of pebbles have dissipated.

And then there are the slight sounds of childhood sliding off as if a camera panning away from a scene. And it was all a movie, and it was all a dream. And the autumn again gives way to winter and to the calm of cold. And the glassy, transparent surface is renewed. I am in the air now. I'm drifting over town as the credits roll. Leaves fall all around me to symbolize the death of a bold love. See my feet sliding over the yellowing-green of ground. See that autumn glow, and the painful paling of color and the smell of maple syrup.

Half of the world fades to black and follows me to the horizon.

And O—there were echoes in her eyes then.

And losing love is so much like waking up suddenly from a dream. It takes a few minutes to realize that the images you just saw weren't real.

I drive away again, still shivering. These are the terms of my unconditional surrender.

chapter five:

Zen Girls and the Hieroglyphs.

Ocean City is an experience all of its own. It comes in late June, and disappears in August. During the rest of the year it is grey black and white photographs, somber seagulls and foamy cliffs. It is cold sand and empty stretches of boardwalk where a thousand shops exist only to wait again for June. In the winter it is a John Wayne ghost town. In the autumn and spring, it is a crippled craft fair. But in those few months in the summer, it is unlike anything your neon dreams could imagine.

Ocean City is a half-hour drive in the off-season. During the summer it can be an hour or more with stop lights, draw bridges, toll booths, traffic jams, and speed traps set up as if we were all pesky roaches, rather than the sparse seasonal air that feeds this ephemeral resort town.

Once you're inside the city limits, no one makes a huge fuss to hold you there. All the hotels and rentals are slum worthy. All the vendors and waitresses are phony. Even the ocean itself is cold and generally narcoleptic.

There are two reasons for this town to exist. One is to watch the opposite sex at their physical peak of tone and tan and nakedness. The other is to drink while doing so.

I drive down at night and meet up with a group of girls I'd met and forgotten about sporadically. The lead one is 5'4" and trim with long shampoo commercial hair and a general air of jubilant normalcy. Of the others, one is constantly talking about films she hadn't seen, one is constantly shivering, and one is always blow drying her hair and complaining about her perfect complexion.

It doesn't seem real that a place like this exists. It seems more like a television show. I'm watching women who belong on television walk around like the rest of us. Only, they don't seem to have as hard a time with the concept of walking as I do. They sort of— float. It's like they belong near an ocean.

The front porch is a revolving door of young men who stop by for five minutes at a time just to remind the girls of their existence. They bring them beer and offer them backrubs, while the women just giggle cunningly and smile their selves free from any attachments.

I sit down with the lead one and six pack, trying to explain existentialism.

"It's so good to have an actual intellectual conversation with someone," she says as she hands me a book called The Complete Idiots Guide to Zen. "I bought this the other day."

I flip through the pages and try to nod politely.

"You know, I've got a lot of great books on this stuff. And I've got friends who have great books that they would be more than willing to lend you…"

"Well, what's wrong with this?"

The one who constantly talks about films walks in and I hold up the book, covering all the words except Idiots and Zen. "Do you think there's anything wrong with this?"

"I've been telling her that all week."

"Oh—go to hell," says the leader. "I wanted something easy to start with. I'm trying, alright damnit."

"You are. I guess that's something. Now where were we?"

"You were explaining existentialism."

"Right. Now what the hell was the definition I

liked? Oh yeah—it says that existence precedes essence. Now what does that mean to you? Existence and essence?"

"Well—it makes me think of being a baby and..."

"Exactly. You're born. You exist."

"Yeah, and I guess—essence is what you make of yourself?"

"Right. So existentialism believes first in free will—in the fact that we aren't born with any predetermined fate, but also that we are responsible for who we are. It's sort of a third take on nature versus nurture. Existentialism almost says neither, that we are who we choose to be, and are thus accountable only to ourselves. Does that make any sense?"

"Yeah..."

The cold one keeps walking back and forth through the house shivering. She is covered in sweatpants and sweatshirts and blankets, but her pale little pixie face and lost little girl eyes peak through and sigh silently. I wish her sadness was deeper than the cold. I could fall for sad eyes any day.

An hour later I excuse myself from the houseful of women who are, in fact, strangely Zen in the way that they deal with the men who bring them beer and offer them backrubs.

Twenty blocks away in a long, smoky bar near the inlet, my father plays keyboard and belts out oddly bluesy renditions of old Led Zeppelin and Doors songs. Behind him, the drummer sits with dark glasses, Billy Idol hair, and a countenance as coolly constant as his rhythm. He raises his hands up and thunders down hard on a black Pearl drum set. His brother stands center stage, bopping up and down on the bass guitar, wearing a blue ball cap over his eyes, and to his right, the long haired slender guitar player kicks and sweeps his fingers with an unconscious sureness across the fret board of a white PRS.

I order a beer and light up a cigarette. The crowd consists mostly of middle-aged couples come out on a Monday night to avoid the doldrums of hotel room basic cable. But the band doesn't mind. They play just as ferociously to ten people as they do to a thousand. They growl out old Rolling Stones songs like Satisfaction and Sympathy for the Devil. They blast through the sonic assault of early U2. They romp over The Who's Won't Get Fooled Again and Baba O'Reilly with mixed animalistic precision and synthesized fury. They growl, scream, muscle, and groove. No one really seems to notice save for the few scattered band loyalists, and the occasional drunken dancers who sway unmusically about the dance floor in provocative posses that never quite fit their aging bodies.

Halfway through the first set, I run into an old friend.

"Fell! Wha's going on man?" Murray slurs and shakes my hand.

"Not a whole lot. Hey—is there anything going on later?"

"Well, we're gonna hit a couple more bars until 2am. After that we'll be on Second Street and Philadelphia. Come on by, man. You'll see us out on the porch."

"Sounds good."

"Alright man. We're going to get some more shots on down the street."

At two, when the bar closes, I move my car down to Second Street and walk around until I see

Murray and two others on the front porch of a large, two story house that hangs out right over the street. Murray is short and stocky, and has a sheep-dog haircut that flops over his eyes and makes him resemble a certain cartoon character. He hands me a beer and introduces the others.

"That's Keith and that's Bill."

"What's going on guys?"

"Not much. Working on that thirty pack."

The night has slowed down considerably. Four hours ago, the streets were brimming with bright-eyed underage girls in underdeveloped outfits looking for wild parties. Now there are only a few sparse cars and street lamps, and the scattered remains of the bars stumbling back to their hotels and condos.

The four of us sit quietly, chain smoking and drinking cheap beer.

I look at Murray, "hey do you have a phone? I might be able to round us up some girls."

"Oh, hell yeah—here."

I call the Zen Girls and get the lead one. I know it's hopeless, but I'd be daft not to try. Anyway, I could use a little television in my life.

There are voices and music blasting in the background.

"Hey, who's this?"

"Hey—it's Charlie. I'm down on Second Street at a pretty happening party." The four of us laugh hard in our throats. "What are you guys doing? Why don't you stop by?"

"Hold on," she cups the receiver, "do you guys want to go to a party on Second? Yeah, we'll probably come. Let me call you back."

"D`you have the number?"

"Yeah, it's on the phone. See you Fell…"

An hour later the phone is still silent. We've opened the second thirty pack and ordered subs from a local all-night shop.

A couple of kids walk by on the street and call up over the balcony in hushed voices, "hey guys—do you mind if we come up there and get high? There're cops all over the streets."

"Hell no. Come on up."

Inside, one of the kids, a thin eighteen year old with wire rimmed glasses, produces a large bag of dope and starts to dissect a cigar.

"We've got a bowl for that, man."

"Oh shit—even better! Thanks."

"Sure."

Their eyes are glassy, and they can't seem to keep still.

"What have you guys been taking?"

"We're rolling."

"Do you have any more of that?"

"Yeah. Hey, do want to buy some?"

Murray studies a handful of purple pills. He turns them over between his fingers and reads the inscription. "Yeah, sure. Keith, Bill, Fell, You guys in?" Keith and I are. We pop the pills over a few more beers and smoke on top of everything else.

At six in the morning, we're all sitting on the porch staring up the white siding overhead. It isn't quite spinning. It looks more like a hieroglyph. The brown water stains are trying to tell us something.

The sun is coming up now. Cars are starting to fill out the streets. Soon there'll be bathing suits lying dead on checkered beach towels while the smell of sun block fills the salty air with its rich coconut musk. Soon there'll be sand castles and hermit crab collectors digging in the sand. And then the bright lights will light up and shine through the sun, and the rides will start spinning.

And the cotton candy will spin. And small children with bloated little bellies will spin around in the cold sea.

And the middle-aged women will sit under their umbrellas reading Cosmopolitan. And the teenage girls will put on their best Zen faces and lure teenage boys into the sea like so many Homeric sirens.

Now we're staring at the white siding overhead. The brown water stains are trying to tell us something.

Keith perks up, "Hey—do you guys think the arcade's open yet?"

"Oh—hell yeah. Let's check it out."

Bill is out cold on the couch, dressed in beer boxes and bottle caps. The rest of us cross the street and walk towards the boardwalk like something out of a zombie movie.

And actually—I don't feel like I'm moving at all. I feel like I'm watching myself. I can't be up this early. It can't be tomorrow, and I can't still be able to walk.

In the morning, the boardwalk is filled with families on family-sized bicycles with three and four wheels. Some lay back, peddle, and shift their weight. Others have canopies and steering wheels.

I used to be one of those kids.

We walk up to the restaurant where Keith works and order a couple of stacks of pancakes and orange juice. The counter girl looks at us cockeyed.

"You fuckers haven't even been to bed yet, have you?"

We haven't.

"Bastards."

We sit on park benches watching the surreal parade of bikes pass us by, like a Dr. Seuss book come to life.   Everyone is jolly and sunny, rested and sped up by coffee and jelly donuts. I look down dumbly at my stack of strawberry pancakes and lift the heavy forkfuls into my mouth in what seems like slow motion. In fact, I feel like I'm underwater. I feel like there must be some easier way to maneuver the world than to walk and grab and jabber. I feel like I could close my eyes and start floating somehow.

The arcades are closed. Everything is becoming hazy and unreadable. The ground is a mirage. It slopes and climbs, stairs and stutters. We stumble back to the house and question the impact of additional beer and dope.

I open one up, but soon find myself lying on the floor, trying to recapture that floating feeling. The sun sneaks in through the blinds over the window, making thin smoky strips of light. I drift off into that.

When I open my eyes again, everyone is gone. I'm lying on the floor, alone, in a strange house. My shoes are a foot away from my feet. I'd reach for them, but my arms are too heavy. I close my eyes again, instead.

I might have walked in on two legs. I'm not quite sure. Something about some pills last night, and a house with six girls, and bar, and then another house.

I wake up on the couch at noon, knowing I haven't slept long. The sun is up. Everyone is marching up and down the streets like they belong in the Macy's Thanksgiving parade. A couple of people in cars and jeeps circle the same two streets like birds on a wire.

Others—women—beautiful young women walk by all wearing the same outfit. They all have the same short shorts and the same tan legs and the same smooth complexion and the same sunken stomach piercing and the same amount of cleavage and the same dark black nondescript sunglass and the same frown. They walk out in the sun in these little outfits that require shoehorns, and they wonder why everyone stares at them. Maybe they walked in on two legs. I'm not quite sure of that either.

Somehow I make it to my car. It's hot and dusty inside, and I can feel the weight of all the cigarettes I smoked last night hanging hard in my lungs.

chapter six:

Epicureanism at Work.

I grew up in the stomach of Alton.

I wasn't born here. In fact, I spent the first few years of my life on the opposite side of the country.

I'm told my father wasn't much of a man. I'm told this, because I don't remember a single fucking detail or event that hasn't been told to me. All I really know is that Vietnam and the bottle had taken care of whatever traces humanity he had.

Father, Mother, and I moved to the east coast to live with my grandparents when I was only a year old. My grandparents lived in a nice European sort of two-story complete with a makeshift vineyard, expansive sunroom, and several oversized photographs of Switzerland.

When I was about two, my grandfather mercifully exiled my father from our lives. He wasn't an abusive man, my father, but he wasn't the sort of person a family could depend on. Truth be told, he hadn't really the capacity take care of himself.

Some might dwell on such exile, such thievery of parentage, or such robbery of the slightest chance of normalcy. But another man came into my life not long after, a better man, a compassionate, warm, and unbearably understanding human being. A real father. A real take you to see *Indian Jones and the Temple of Doom*, buy you a *happy meal*, running through the woods on a week-day with a German shepherd, playing catch in the backyard father.

We moved to Alton not long after where he taught high school and some college before, upon the advice of his artistic and emotional mentor, he abandoned those more noble and safe positions to follow his heart into a career as a musician. Not long after, he and my mother separated.

In the short time they were married he legally adopted me as his own son. And unlike the first man in my life to hold the title of father, he never abandoned me. Twenty years later, he still hasn't.

My mother, on the other hand, put her background in theatre to good use and became a realtor. We lived for a long time in the hollow belly of Alton, moving sporadically, but always ending up in those in-between neighborhoods where the adults might bring you fruit baskets and borrow a cup of sugar, and the kids might steal your bike. We even had a couple of neighbors who'd set traps for our cat or call social services to report on the indignity in which I was raised. But if these were Puritans, subjects of senility, or concerned truths, I'm not altogether sure. To tell you the truth, most of my childhood is a complete haze. And that frightens me more than anything.

Years later, following a successful succession of marriages, my mother and I moved into one of those houses that line the great V which spreads out across the edges of Alton. Now, she lives there in a world of golf courses and minivans. She vacations in quiet beach communities, adopts foreign children and wears the color pink with frightening consistency. It's still strange to see her, who used to be the archetypal struggling working mother, living here along the arms of the V.

I still see her often, stopping by for sandwiches and loans that I'll probably never pay back. I suppose she's not exactly happy with who I am, or what I'm doing. But the thing is—I've never really been—I don't know—ordinary. I've never really wanted to be.

But I get the distinct feeling that's exactly what she's always been desperate to become.

Mother calls me on a Saturday and asks if I can housesit for a week while she and the husband vacation in a quiet beach community. She always likes to wait until the last minute to ask, because she knows I'll always do it, and she knows the less advance I get, the fewer plans I can make to take advantage of the luxuries her house provides.

Sunday.

I walk in near midday and check for notes, directions, warnings, threats, and money for groceries.
Once I'm satisfied the coast is clear, I unload the car and deposit ashtrays on all the tables, a drum set in the corner of the downstairs living room, and several cases of beer in the bar beside the stairwell.
The first floor is slightly underground and highly soundproof. Its living room extends across the entire embankment on one side. To the right is a game room with a pool table and various other diversionary treasures. To the left lies the guest bathroom and bedroom, which weaves wooden floors out onto the lower deck and spa.
Over this, unfinished stairs lead upwards to the wide, white glowing kitchen and piano room, three bedrooms, two baths, office, dining, and second living room. I unroll books and notepads onto a desk, and then walk out to the deck to smoke and await the dusk.
Beneath me is a long, narrow sloping yard that unravels and arches like a cat. Currents of lush green grass reach downhill to a shallow stream, just wide enough for a small canoe. On the way down beaming birds bounce off of trapdoor feeders hanging from

weeping lemon trees.

Cigarettes burn slower here. Time rolls like summer sap. Depth is drowned in privilege.

Near midnight the first flickers of laughter echo up the unfinished stairs. Tim and Sid emerge with wide grins, followed shortly by Stephen, Simeon and three women. The first, Hani, is short and rather stout, but pleasant. Her deep earthen eyes and easy smile save her figure somewhat. Beside her an exceedingly average girl stands quietly and invisibly over-polite. Behind her, arching and over-posing is Crystal, who is everything a name endows. She is beautiful, shimmering in sun bleached hair and fair skin, and awarded with affable eyes and thick vermilion lips that curl and part in the ever-present laughter of her light spirit. She is as beautiful and deep as new glass.

Outside the shiny thing speaks—

"...no really, I scare off a lot of men. I guess I'm a bit overzealous, or—too direct. Guys get so attached that they never understand that I just want something around every now and then."

Her eyebrows bend downwards in bright laughter at seeing all our eyes blink open at attention.

I jump up first. "Hi, I'm Charlie. Nice to meet you. Want to go for a swim?" She giggles and runs after her bathing suit.

Soon eight figures make their way downstairs into the hot tub. The girl is indeed lovely. Two small pieces of fabric cover her exquisitely pale parts, exposing the flat stomach struck with only a hint of childhood. She lingers on the side with her legs dangling miniature feet into everyone's laps secretly underwater.

The sky over us is clear and raining with light

from thousands of years ago. And we, simple creatures below, sit unaware of anything but this moment, this time, this life.

Stephen produces a joint. Time passes. Water lulls and caresses. Air dries. Grass leans over in the evening chill. Somewhere little cats pounce behind clandestine boxwoods.

Lightning bugs flash in trees like moveable stars. Trees sway fingers but stiffen thick wooden thighs. Minds wander with light wind, wondering what is possible on a night like this where eyes caress dripping body parts in the dim glow of natural nightlight.

No real words pass. No moments of epiphany reach us except that smoke and whiskey sting, her flesh, and my ideas.

Only—

"Do you live around here? Really!"

"Yeah, you know…"

"Another one?"

(exhale—)

"Huh."

"Really?"

"Uh huh."

Five men are unaware. Three women are unaware. Only the distant light is aware of the inevitable end of harmony. For now we are all one vast body, one form.

Lola Thomas appears in the distant shadows shinning the sorrow in her eyes like it was a flashlight or flare gun. She is a cadaver. She looks and smells like a cadaver.

She gets in and drifts my way despite the absurd, puzzled looks of the accumulated crowd. Just then, all the secret underwater foot dances die.

Now I wish something drastic—a vaudeville exit for a maudlin entrance. Something like a cat with no legs. Something that wants to be funny, but becomes only irreversibly sad.

I eye my gin and tonic with some distrust. And then I swallow it whole.

"I'm going to get another."

"I'll come with you."

I know what she wants. I know exactly what she wants. The alcohol has enlightened me. I pull her into the bathroom and tear off her clothes. At least she's still warm to the touch.

We fall on the narrow floor and start thrusting dumbly at each other, but there isn't enough room.

"Ouch! Charlie!"

"Come on…"

We peer into the hallway. The coast is clear.

I throw her towel on the floor of the guest room. She starts giggling now.

I can't let her see my face. I used to dream about this girl. I used to elevate her. She used to be marble in my mind. Now my stomach is fighting back.

I move on, stiffly, despite the lump in my throat. And I finish what feels like necrophilia and pull out of her.

I can't let her see my face.

Lola dresses to leave.

Downstairs someone's stomach grumbles.

"Oh! I can go to the store," says the shimmering thing. "But it closes in a half-hour! Everyone give me money…"

We all throw small bills at her, and she runs off still half undressed and dripping in her small suit at nearly two in the morning.

The remainder then files slowly in, claiming couches and instruments, or else beer and breakfast cereals.

Two minutes later Crystal runs in, sobbing and hysterical.

"I locked my keys in! And the car is running! And you're all hungry, and I still have to drive two-hundred miles tonight! And…and…" Her little lips shake miserably and her little forehead wrinkles as if they belonged to a small child who has just lost its favorite toy.

All the men suddenly become extraordinarily empathetic, singing, "there, there honey. It'll be alright…" It's funny to watch everyone talk to their dinner.

She phones a serviceman as we all inspect her car, hoping for the sword in the stone, or the discovery that will earn our respective knighthood. Even I become the eager diver in the shallow stream.

An hour later a truck arrives, fills out fifteen forms, produces a tool, mends and disappears.

"Oh! Thank you! I love you so much!" The girl chants to our collective disaffection.

Tim and I have the last words with her, insisting on future phone calls and better parties with happier endings.

"Oh definitely! D`you have a pen? Oh—Oh well, get my number from Hani. Goodbye. Goodbye!"

Tim and I have a cigarette on my car top. Our eyes roll backwards as we erupt in laughter.

This is only the beginning.

Monday.

Good mornings always open around noon. There're only twelve hours now to deal with the blankets, bodies, bottles, cellophane, cigarettes, drumsticks, glasses, guitars strings, hammers, lighters, lost socks, matchbooks, shirts, swimsuits, stains, towels, television and lost underwear.

But all this is easily done by the aid of dishwashers, washing machines, and lemon-scented cleaning agents. I abscond instead to the deck and claim a small spot in the shade to read.

Amory Blaine is discovering Shelly, Shaw, and socialism among the boughs of Princetonian oaks and spires. Meanwhile, I wash up every day in the same small town, wondering when and where these kinds of happenings will return. It feels like we're all waiting, hoping for some great straw to stir and unsettle the saccharine ease with which we have emerged at the end of the 20th century in a slumber worthy of Yeats' The Second Coming.

Sometimes I imagine myself doing well, like I'm diving in the fog just to collect upon the relics of my day. I imagine the artist's purpose must be to represent faithfully his surroundings, or to always be the fool looking up. I imagine myself as possessing an arcane timelessness, arising as an abstruse anomaly belonging to no one man, culture, creed or age. For now I am I gatherer of personages, but secretly, I am a harbinger of change. All this and more lives buried neatly within the arrogance of my youth.

Stones roll, air breathes for Mother Earth; little currents form and pass, will and change. Time is a vicious part of everything, relentless in its dissipation of the past and ruthless in its preservation of the future.

The second night is nowhere near as lively as the first. Rather, it is an eerie calm in the center of the inevitable hurricane to come. Tim, among the only attendants, is to be the only permanent figure of the evening. His spirits are still high today, and he is peaceful. I imagine this as well to be the uneven serene swell of a temporary center.

Tonight we trade company in numbers for numbers of vices. A thick mushroom cloud of smoke engulfs and wills us into submission. All now is to the sound of the beat, the breath of the music, and the thrill of carrying a rhythm into a textural flurry. Tim strums wildly on his new upright bass as I follow with a trance of cymbals, kick and snare.

Over the mantle hang symbolic pictures, pottery, and pretension. We feel like thieves playing under a temple, or hustlers in churches of upper middle class religions designed and followed out in careful formulas. Underneath all this sit the purveyors of abstract jazz, stoned and aloof of the lawyers, doctors, and bemused businessmen encircling us at all angles. Occasionally we look upwards and laugh. But mostly, we wander on dressed only in our instruments.

Two roads divulged in a wood. And we take the beaten path. But once inside, we dig deep trenches, light fires and wait.

Tuesday.

The usual crowd comes in near midnight. Timothy and Sid have already been working the pool table for over an hour when Ethan enters with a suitcase of jazz records and an overlarge straw hat that gives off the impression of a displaced character from a Mark Twain novel.

"Hey," he speaks in a slow thoughtful manner,

"thought you could pr'haps use some music."

"Put in on, man. You want a drink?"

"I wouldn't be adverse to that."

Ethan is the old man of the group at twenty-five. The extra years are obvious in both the concentration of his eyes (revealed by oft-raised brows) and by the colloquial, but deeply thoughtful manner in which he replies to all of our bemused inquiries. Any other man would seem slightly condescending, saying these sort of things. But Ethan's stoical and painfully earnest nature makes his most threatening rebukes seem like mild honesty.

Timothy walks in.

"What's the matter, man?"

"I've just had a bad day, that's all. My father is holding it against me that I'm 'being aloof' as if every mode of contact has to come from me. I'm his son, goddamnit! It's as much his responsibility as mine."

"..."

"And work was no better…"

"Listen man," Ethan says, "I hope you're not going to complain like this every time we hang out."

"I didn't mean to…"

"That's alright. We all have problems. But it does us no use dwelling on such things."

And whereas another would've ignited Tim into a fury of retribution, Ethan evokes a simple shrug, and a—

"Yeah, maybe."

Ethan and I make drinks and carry them into the hot tub. The water inside warms what the air relinquished at sundown. And above, and all around, the children of summer have come out to play in neat swarms of flashing fire and erratic buzzing.

Soon after, Stephen appears with Simeon and his little sister Larissa, who is giggling uncontrollably. I motion for them to change and join us.

Larissa is just eighteen, and is one of those late blooming beauties who've hid their noses too long indoors dreaming, or else in televisions asleep. You can tell instantly that her mind still has far to go to catch up with her body, lean and bulging in strategically sound places. Her lips hang dumbly from her pretty face, and her eyes have all the light and width of fireflies.

Seeing her, Ethan's eyes roll so far back into his head that laughter would be completely inappropriate. Fear—or at best complacent outrage is ringing in his eyes. Had I not the drinks in me sufficient to forgive simplicity for smooth thighs, I might have to agree. But I am in no mood for being respectable. The game is out and I have the biggest gun.

She slides in alone on the far corner and commences to splash at me playfully, her childlike little fingers rolling along the top of the water. Looking closely, you can see a half-cracked smile where the woman is leaking from the girl.

I return fire, and get a giggle and a foot up my ankle. Then the little imp leaps over to me and tackles my midsection, flailing wildly until she ends perched prettily on my lap.

"Hey!" she shrieks as Ethan exhibits a sad smile in his still corner. It's to him as if the museum has been closed, and in its place erected a munitions warehouse. But she only splashes on. Fire, leap and tackle.

Simeon appears sporadically to eye us with deep disapproval. Failing each time, he only retreats inside.

Stephen is long gone. Even Ethan eventually tires of trying to save me and follows the rest in. Now I and the little imp are alone in the water, striving to decide who is to be the shark and who the swimmer.

"You're simple," she giggles mercilessly. By now I've pulled her in the middle where the water is deepest. Her smooth little legs wrap around my waist as I catch her eyes.

"Simple? How am I simple?"

"You just are."

My thoughts are simple. My thoughts, at this moment in time, could not be any simpler.

She looks straight through me. "You're simple," she repeats as we drift closer.

As I kiss her, my spare hand sheds her skin like a snake's, and out slivers the subdued woman within.

There's a bed just inside the doorway. We dress for it after finding our clothes, swum into the filter.

Inside she sheds again. But her body has become somehow stiff and rigid. Her limbs and her lips are tender, but her middle and insides are frozen.

"I've never done this before…" she whispers. And then my body becomes stiff and rigid as well.

This is a gift, this is sinister, this is what she wants, this is what I want, this is the guilt talking, this is my most primal defense, this is not my problem, this is hers to give, this is the only time, this is a pathetic fantasy, this is a ball of light, this is your conscience, this is the whiskey speaking, this is my humanity, this is her body, this happens every day, this is something— this is something I can't be.

She counters, "it's okay. I mean, I want to…"

"No. No, I can't. I'm sorry, I can't do this." I look up at her. "Save this. Save this for someone who deserves it." I hand her her clothes and move myself to the safe side of the bed. She is inevitably shocked. She is still and speechless. I stand up and move for the door.

"But…but I want—"

"Go home." I close the door behind me.

Tim and Sid are on their way out onto the porch to smoke.

"Mind if I join you?"

"Hey…" Tim cracks a wild grin and holds up his right hand. I half slap it.

"I didn't do anything. It would've been her first. I couldn't…"

"Yeah? That's cool." He pauses and cracks a smile, "but you could've…"

Larissa spots Sid from below the deck. I back into a corner so as not to be seen.

"Where's Simeon? I've got to get home, it's sooo late."

"Is he your ride?"

"No. I just—how do I get out of here?"

"You can follow me to the bypass. I'm leaving now. I'll be right down"

Sid says goodbye as Tim and I gasp for air and choke back our amusement.

But I'm not all amused. Part of me is scared for something that didn't happen, or maybe for something that will. Or maybe for the is that will never be, or for the girl that will always be wasn't.

Part of me that is disappointed that I didn't act.

Something just outside of nothing is happening here. That is all. We roll no stones but for time and distance.

Wednesday.

In the morning I am alone again, despite my worst efforts, and I find myself confronted with a certain sense of regret at what my actions are initiating in others. She was a fucking kid, a child. And, although I see myself causing no real long term disruption in her life, she has certainly caused a temporary one in mine, if only to call into question where my motives have gone.

Besides that there are the abstruse actions of others at this place, and in this environment that I have provided. To me, a room and a noise, drugs and their beneficiaries should inspire more than the empty pursuit of intellectually dead women. And perhaps (or of course) I am being naïve, or old, or idealistic. But either way, I'm waking up with disappointment and stale beer on my breath.

By day I find myself returning to old books already read, looking naively for those sparks that incited the first fires of creativity, or purity, or at least a vaguely artful shade of interest. But ironically, I am increasingly finding myself less resembling those literary traits of the writers, and more so resembling the affluence and arrogance of the characters to which they wrote so eloquently and so condescendingly.

On one shoulder I imagine this sort of immersion into madness and recklessness to be an entirely necessary part of the growth of my understanding. On the other, I see the withering away of those things which make a man capable of the levels of remorse and empathy that are essential to the creation of anything. I need to stop the spinning. I need something drastic. I need a symbol, a harbinger, an innocence. I need a clear reminder that while good and evil exist on a level of balances—good is the preferable experience.

Philosophy can be stoned. Love can be drunk. Innocence can experience. But we are making no movements here besides the sideways slivering of snakes.

And maybe it's naïve to expect depth from a crowd. And maybe my cast is flawed. Maybe we're all too young.

Or maybe we're all too old. Maybe everyone here has outgrown their imaginations. Romance doesn't come in dollhouses anymore. We're expected to deal with this. We're expected to grow up and get jobs. We're expected to watch our children run around in their own dollhouses. And we're never expected to ask why.

Maybe we're simply rebelling the only way we have left. Age has taken our innocence and stolen our ability to dream. But we still have our bodies, and we still have the chemicals to deceive them. And this is what we're to think being young is about. And who is to argue when pleasure replaces enlightenment. This, after all, is the American way.

Stephen enters with armfuls of alcohol—gin, rum, tequila, vodka, and triple sec. And this is to be the night of the long island ice tea.

The long island ice tea is the drink that does for madness what gasoline does for a car, or sunlight to a garden. The mixture is quick, flavorful and secretive in its strength. Soon we've enveloped several entering strangers within our various parades of music, pool tables, chain-smoking, hot tubs, canoe rides, and deck discussions.

And then Cassandra appears. Cassandra is small, but her undersized frame is made up for by the over pronouncement of all her features. Her hair is a golden wave, and her eyes are jade Venetian waterways. Bright cheekbones pull full lips even higher and wider. Her waistline is nonexistence save for the inward slope that becomes fully extended into graceful miniature feet on one end, and that wrap around into the full portions of her breast on the other.

Her expression possesses the cunning and calculated knowledge of the accumulated affect of her features. And her countenance, which might appear sinister if sober, becomes in this state what sirens were to mythical sailors.

Slightly behind her is a young male companion who appears completely dumbfounded by the whole experience.

"You know you're the first person in history to use this door?"

"Oh really? I'm sorry, I just thought it would make a much better entrance."

No one has noticed her yet. The others are far too scattered to be either interested or threatening. But had they seen her, no doubt would they have tried to prolong this sort of stalled conversation in a vain attempt to attain her interest.

But this is not the sort of girl to be impressed by affable politeness. Fire is attracted to fire. One shiny object deserves another.

"Did you bring a bathing suit?"

"Yeah. I'm wearing it underneath."

"Good. Let's go."

Outside I produce a cigarette, submerge, and do my best at looking aloof and comfortable inside the bubbling water. Less than a minute later the girl strolls down the long wooden steps, now undressed, revealing all my imagination had previously procured.

I light and hand her a smoke, and she doesn't waste a second.

"So we were at this party last night—right—and this friend of mine was asking what my opinion was of oral sex in public places." *Look left, nod, exhale.* "I told him, if a guy's got the balls to whip it out, then the girl should have the guts to suck it."

I don't know whether to laugh or cheer or run. "What'd he say?"

"Nothing. He just turned completely white."

"I guess he wasn't expecting that."

"I guess not…"

At this her companion limps awkwardly down the stairs.

She continues, "so anyway…"

I drift off. Good and evil are subjective things when blended in a bottle. Stir youth in hot water and you'll quickly see decency submerge. I have found the brightest marble, the most attractive toy. My hands are enjoying its edges underwater. Had not the clock fingers as well—

"Shit—what time is it? I've got to get to Summer's house. She'll fucking kill me…" (to her companion) "Can you get my things inside?"

In the driveway we are alone. "Are you going to be around later?"

"Yeah, probably..."

"I'll probably come back then." She exhales smoke when she speaks. "Summer won't *need* me too long…"

Her little body leans into mine gently and I wrap my arms around her. "I'll be back—"

But I know better. Her power would be diminished if I hadn't the time to stir her around in my brain while her body is absent. I know this is all part of the game, and I am not so naïve as to be disappointed by her disappearance.

Inside there are mountains of bodies made by

Stephen's mixture. Some stiff carcass occupies every inch of couch and chair, and every base of every television.

Upstairs Tim and Sid pace the kitchen in a hollow daze. The faint sound of their laughter gives them away. I join them for a while.

Soon, I myself become a cadaver on some couch in front of some television.

Thursday.

Ethan appears at a sliding glass door just outside the kitchen.

"What've you got going on in here, man? What happened to the cook-out?"

"We were a little short on fuel."

Laughing, "so now you're cooking for forty, eh? Boy they got you good."

"Yeah…"

"Well…you want a hand"

"Sure…"

Ethan drops a grocery bag and a small wooden box covered in chipped olive-green paint onto a chair by the table. From the box, he produces a pile of cds, which are then promptly escorted to the nearest stereo. Once this is done, he rolls up his sleeves and becomes entirely serious. "What am I doing?"

I hand him a cutting board and a few cloves of garlic.

"You any good with sauces?"

"I don't know. I might be…"

We stand over a stewing pot with a series of wooden spoons and wrinkled foreheads. And then, as if in a burst of cartoon light bulbs, Ethan marches towards the spice rack, and I for the wine. And then it becomes sport to throw, sprinkle, pitch, pour, pause, taste, ponder, shake, shower, salt, pepper, wine, garlic, sugar, basil, red pepper, oregano, black pepper, celery salt, garlic, spoons, furled brows, more sugar…

"Ah! Victory!"

"Now you have to let it simmer, man—bring out its *essence*." Ethan's pronunciation is determinedly absurd. We pause to consider this before bursting into laughter.

Next I brown the chicken and shave flakes of parmesan from a block. Ethan, at the cutting board, brandishes a butcher knife over a pile of lettuce, tomatoes, cucumbers, carrots, and peppers. The kitchen is strewn with the skins of vegetables, wrappers, plastic bags, bottles, cans, cutlery, containers, pots, pans, packages, aluminum foil and saran.

All the while various party patrons wander in and out of the kitchen, searching blankly for their mislaid beers or bottles of whiskey.

"Out! Out! Damn you!"

The dinning room table is still filled with relics from family. I free them to a foreign piano bench and hunt out matching chairs. Within fifteen minutes we've set the table with chicken, two kinds of tortellini with three kinds of cheese, salad, wine, bread, condiments, butters, dips, powders, and Ethan's broiled fish.

A pipe is produced and smoked as if in pre-dinner prayer. Cassandra and her moderately baked companion sit on my right, while Ethan mans my left. Opposite us is a revolving door of diners, scrambling for silverware, stuffing and absconding.

"Wow…hmpphh…mmphh…hhh….(cough)….great…"

Upstairs we savor and enjoy. Downstairs they

are dancing and sharpening allegorical pool sticks for watery women. I can hear Stephen's heh-he-heh laugh, Tim's imaginary words, and an unknown girl arguing over the lull of guitars on a portable stereo.

Outside it is quiet and cool. The sky is washed black save for the incorruptible stars shimmering silently.

Cassandra produces a pair of cigarettes.

"So that was pretty impressive. Who d`we have to thank for that feast?"

"Ethan and I…"

"Mostly him," Ethan says wryly, sneaking up behind us.

"Wow. A real nineties man…" she says exhaling smoke.

"Wrong decade."

"What?"

"Fuck! Wrong century."

Ethan leans against the unsteady wooden rail and rolls his eyes inwardly. I know he won't approve unless she's got an ocean underneath those eyes.

No ocean. A golden pond, pr'haps. A sleek and shimmering state of metallic posing. Tonight, I am a man for metal—

We board a canoe in the backyard, and Cassandra settles below me with her back between my legs. Her head leans backwards into my lap.

The water beneath us replicates the sky, and a canopy of trees stretch out from the shore to hover over us.

Her hair is a blonde velvet waterfall. Her skin is tender and easy, welcoming even to old hands.

Inside her rests regeneration. So what if it's only of the body? What after all is the mind without its vehicle? What peace is there for paintings when I can't sleep or eat of love?

I eat poorly, rarely and unevenly. I sleep only hours a night. And all too often I fall in love with the brush before the canvas. But what of it? Twenty two and nothing is real.

But this is nothing new either. Any hack philosopher with a dime bag knows this—

"This is beautiful Charlie. Just look at the sky— it's so clear, and quiet…"

Yes. Look at the sky. I am large, I contain multitudes.

There are no ghosts in these people. There's no gold either, but at least the ghosts are gone for a while.

I find my hands on her, from summer wheat down to shoulders and slender sides. She leans back and receives my fingers into her soft epicurean skin. She's talking about another party filled with people I'll never meet. I do my best to convince her I'm interested.

Overzealous frogs croon single notes in deep voices that obscure their size. Sneaking fish leap up and alarm, all in a harmony of nature. Everything here possesses a life and yet none of nothing is aware of its soul. None of it is burdened. Here everything functions without so much need for depth. Here life never ceases to surge, and still it never stops to wonder why.

I lose the girl again once we hit the shore.

"I'll probably see you later," she blinks before disappearing into a shiny sports car.

"I'll hold my breath…"

Tim and Sid are up four games to three over Lois and Lorelei. Tim is visibly drunk.

"Charlie! Hey! Watchoo—watchoo been doing?"

"Not much. I went out on the water for a while."

"Wow. We've been playing poooool. Hahaha. Poooool. Hahahaha…"

"Yeah, that's great man," backing away.

"The—the last game…" moving forward.

"Uh huh…" moving away.

"I hit the cue ball and…" cornering.

"Yeah…" trapped.

"It went over the side and it almost hit Hid in the sead—uh—Sid in the head!"

"Wow…" stepping away.

"And then…"

Lois is tucked under Sid's arm in the corner. Lorelei is opposite, alone. I free myself from Tim to have a closer look.

"Hey, you're Charlie, right? Nice place."

"Thanks. It's not mine, though. I'm just house sitting. Hey, d`you want a drink?"

"That would be great…"

Ethan is upstairs admiring the mess.

"You thinking about cleaning this any time soon?"

"Not really. Not tonight. I figure I'll get it in the morning."

"Sounds good to me, man. What's on downstairs?"

"You know those old men in bars—the ones in the bad, grease-stained clothes who drink too much and then accost strangers, the whole time standing about this far away from your face and talking unintelligibly about things you'd never understand anyway?"

Big grin, "yeah…"

"That's Tim."

"Awwwuhh! Let's go!"

Ethan furls his eyebrows seriously, and aims an odd shot into the corner. The cue moves slowly, but steadily into the three, which drops in the pocket.

Lorelei makes me a seat next to her on a little red bench. Her auburn skin spills from small white shorts in thin, smooth shafts. Her body is lean and made a little menacing by sharp, slanted eyebrows. I can tell something is coming.

Her next shot is wide right. But she makes up on defense, obscuring my shot with her outstretched body. I try to straddle her, shooting between her arm and the crescent curve of her side. No good.

Next I lean in front of her, holding her waist level as she leans sideways. She covers me again, and again I miss. I make a mocking move toward the bra strap hanging outside of her tank top.

"Hey!" She backs away playfully. "No one's ever been able to do that with one hand..."

Ethan sinks the eight and proceeds to empty the pockets for a new game.

Tim is standing in the middle of the kitchen among the aftermath of dinner, looking like he belongs with the empty pans and plates.

"Tim..."

His shirt is off, and his left hand is busy clawing savagely at his side as if it were seeking air.

"Tim, what's the matter?"

Dryly, "I don't know."

"Did something happen tonight?"

"It's just that..." whispering, "everyone's against me. All of them. It—never—stops..."

"Tim..."

"I can hear them. They won't go away." His eyes are the eyes of a child.

"Tim—hey Tim—look at me. Tim, do me a favor. Go lie down on the couch for awhile. Tim?"

"I can't sleep. It's just no use anymore. I CAN'T!" His fists are serious, pounding the truth out on tabletops. His hands hit inanimate objects with the impossible clarity of a child.

"Tim—just try. Please. Just try."

He thunders over sullenly to the couch, closes his eyes, and falls asleep right away.

Outside a new day is rising. I look over to Lorelei—

"There's a little stream outback that winds around the neighborhood. D`you want to go for a canoe ride, maybe catch the sunrise?"

"Yeah, sure…"

I steer, letting her talk about herself as much as possible. She works night shifts and often doesn't go to bed until midmorning. She just got a new car and is going back to school. She is fairly responsible without being in control, clever without being too deep.

"Men are afraid of me," she says, "I guess I'm too direct…"

"No—not you. It's not like you'd straddle a complete stranger over a pool table."

She grins at this. Her mouth reaches wide despite her thin face.

Behind the girl a new day is dawning. I know this is no metaphor for my growth. I know this girl is nothing muse worthy, and she knows I'm not looking for that sort of connection.

By this the game grows.

Lavish landscapes creep up all around. Lush green yards and aspirin-white houses litter the

background. Rows of little ducks are chased off
shorelines by over-groomed cats. The occasional SUV
purrs awake and speeds off to a nearby private school.
And I, and a girl, miles away from home or sleep or
sobriety, row stealthily along the streams running
through their backyards.

Back at the house, we claim a bedroom upstairs
and watch cartoons beneath the curtain of a coffee-
colored quilt. Courage caught, I cradle her head
sideways with my right arm. Her lips open, and her
body becomes instantly eager.

Thin legs wrap around me like the blade of a
trap. I lift her up slightly and with my right index and
thumb undo her bra. Her eyes light up.

"Do you have one?"

"Yeah—hold on…"

I dash downstairs and free a strip of condoms
from a cabinet beneath the bathroom sink. A minute
later she cradles me back into position before a hail of
shed clothing. Save for two places, her body is
completely hairless and smooth.

We become like water. She spins me over until
she's satisfied in each new position. Over. Over.

With no breath left, we collapse and roll into a
heavy sleep.

Friday.

Two hours later the kitchen stirs.

"Shit—that's probably Lois." Lorelei peeks into
the hall, half dressed. "Ahh! I don't think that's Lois!"

I get dressed and have a look. The cleaning lady
stands dumbfounded in the kitchen amid an ineffable
pile of leftovers.

"Hey—I—I didn't think you were coming this

week…"

"Yeah. I'm here." she says, pretending to be calm.

"Look—this is too much—this isn't your problem. I was planning on doing this anyway. Why don't you take the day off?"

"Hell, I'll take a day off. No problem." She packs her things quickly and makes for the door downstairs.

"You've been paid already, right?"

"Yup, last week."

"Great. Look—I'm really sorry about all this."

"Hey, that's alright. I'm going home. It's no problem." She steps halfway through the door. "This never happened, right?"

"Yeah. Thanks."

"That was the cleaning lady." Lorelei and I explode into laughter.

"What did she say?"

"Nothing, I sent her home. I think she was happy to have the day off."

We catch our breath before going back to sleep.

When we wake a few hours later Lois's car appears in the driveway.

Lorelei walks downstairs to look for her friend, and appears a minute later, giggling wildly.

"Charlie, something's in the bedroom. Come look."

She coaxes me into knocking. A minute later, there is a loud, masculine cough, and then Sid and Lois appear red-faced from the hallway.

After they leave, I sweep and dispose of everything. Mind, body, floor, counter, table, porch, shower, and bedroom. And for the first time, the silence feels genuinely healthy.

There are pictures of me hung down narrow dark hallways. Some of the pictures are laughing on the beach, or rolling in the ocean. Others are glossy black and white studio shots with sullen hard eyes too old for five. These are the hardest to look at. The motivation for misery must have been drastically different at that age. But the eyes are exactly the same.

Tim turns up on the porch door wearing his eyes.

"Come on in man. How are you doing?"

"I feel—better. I just can't do that anymore Charlie." He looks up at me with the frustrated eyes of a child. "I can't drink anymore. It's—it's not working. It's not working anymore."

"I know—good. I know…"

"I'm sorry about last night, I…"

"It's alright, man. I know. But like you said, it's not working."

"Yeah…"

"Are you on call tonight?"

"Yeah. Actually, I have to go there now. I hope everything will be—I mean—I think it will. Be fine."

"Are you…"

"I just feel like crashing now. I don't know. It never ends Charlie. Everything is repeating, and I can't—I can't break out of it. It's just no use. It's not working anymore…"

"…"

"I guess I'll be back."

"Yeah. I'll see you…"

There is nothing I can say. I can trust that life has the ability to sustain itself. But that's all.

Sometimes men move through wars with will

alone to keep them alive. And maybe there's less to fight for now. And maybe there's less to win. Maybe man has become understated by reaching for such singular victories—companions and a roof—or a lover and a bed—or a meal and a vehicle.

There are no more wars for honor or freedom. And maybe satisfaction is splintered by interest. And maybe Tim is simply disinterested.

Stay alive, old friend—

Cassandra arrives alone a little after ten. She again produces a pair of cigarettes and proceeds to muse over what a wild week she's had here and abroad.

And then an old figure appears, walking up those wooden stairs. And Cassandra and I grimace visibly.

"Hey Low."

Lola Thomas is a pale apparition on the porch.

"Charlie. You haven't called in a while…"

"No? I hadn't realized. I guess I've been a little busy here."

"Oh, I'm sure. Hello Cassandra."

"…"

Hello old ghost.

She must see me here now and imagine how low I've sunk.

Maybe I am taking her for granted. But—it seems too easy. It feels too tranquil. It offers too effortless an ending. I know I could be with her again. I know I could sit in that bedroom with her every night. I know I could have a warm body again, every night. I know I could have human intentions. But it all seems too easy now.

We fit without going anywhere—like old explorers who settled on the first shoreline they saw. I can't do that anymore. I want to go west. I want to go further. I want to dig for gold and dry up in dustbowls. I want to discover Mexico and strike oil. I want to invent the wheel and the light bulb, or die with a heart of gold and a stomach full of stories. Or die trying. Die American.

There is something so sinister in that girl, and not the same sort of sinister that Cassandra's selling. With her it's blatant and thus rendered immaterial. She is designed for such things. With Lola, it's the warmth that becomes sinister. It's the comfort, security, stillness, and the ominous immobility.

Cassandra senses the weight in the air.

"I have to go…"

"Yeah. I'll walk you down."

Lola leans against the rail imagining herself aloof enough to not notice.

"Thanks for stopping by…"

"Yeah. Good luck Charlie. Maybe I'll be back later."

"Yeah—maybe. Goodbye."

Upstairs.

"So—was I interrupting anything?"

"Not that I know of…"

"Oh, come on. You two looked like you were about to attack each other."

"I don't know…"

"Well—d`you want to get in the hot tub?"

"There's no one here Lola. I'm not getting in alone."

"I'm here."

"Yeah, well—you shouldn't be…"

Tim and Sid appear at the stairs just then. Tim is a good soldier. He stands between the tension and talks about nothing.

And then Dean Malarkey and his brother Seth, bearded and wild-eyed, emerge at the top of the stairs.

"Hey Charlie! Oh god, that's not who I think it is..."

"Hello Dean. Remember me?"

"Hey Lola. Sure, sure. Hey Fell, is this it tonight?"

"Afraid so. You caught the winding down of a wild week."

"Ain't that my luck? Hey, where can I put this?"

I show him to the guest room upstairs.

"Man, what is she doing here?"

"She just kind of shows up now. There's no telling when."

"Really? Well let's have some fun then…"

Downstairs Dean mans a heavy upright bass with long limber fingers. He is cool and complacent there, the opposite of his brother. He is clean cut, sober, sharp-witted, and fast.

Seth is outwardly quiet and rather subdued. But behind his long hair and bright red beard there is something caged that comes out sharply whenever provoked.

He stands strong on guitar, shaking his tall muscular frame sideways to the beat. I play evenly on drums behind them, but Dean pulls the groove. His heavy hand leads a bass line like no one else I've ever seen. He defies all boundaries of age and race, thumping something that is at once violent and primal and entirely smooth and mechanical.

Tim stands beside him, transfixed for a moment before becoming entirely frustrated at his own inabilities to produce such sounds. Sid joins him in the game room. Lola is lurking somewhere.

When we break for drinks, I hear Dean upstairs
on Lola.

"Let me get this straight—he broke up with
you, and yet you still hang around? Do you sleep with
him? Do you have any idea what you're doing? Do
you have any fucking self respect at all?"

"…"

"I know you never liked me little girl. You
know I never liked you much either."

"Yeah—fuck you Dean! Fuck you! You always
were a fucking asshole. Thanks for reminding me."

Laughing, "Yeah! That's it! Wake up! Let it
out! You're nowhere little girl. You're fucking
nowhere…"

But she's somewhere. She is here. Drink
enough and wherever you are exists. She knows this,
and she lies and waits.

Dean and Seth gag and get a game of pool.
Dean is waiting for his girl. Tim and Sid split early.

I give in eventually, and I go to bed with Lola.

She holds on tight, but I never move but to stay
warm and wait for morning.

Saturday.

I've been hearing about this girl Grace for a
while. Althea mentioned her briefly. She said she was
literary, philosophical, religious and musical. And I
remember seeing her in a play once. I remember
watching the way she moved—warmly and with a
delicate kindness, a well of humor, and an honest and
affable charm.

Althea gave me her number before she left, but

I'd waited a while to call her. Even when I did, I ended up leaving messages that got no reply.

I actually spent a decent amount of time sitting around and staring at the phone, wanting to make it ring until it became this mythical sort of impossibility. I'd attached an importance to her above everything else.

Maybe she really is the only muse worthy woman around. Or maybe I'm just imagining things. Either way, the phone is heavy in my hands. Either way, it's harder to talk to a poet than a dancer.

Then one day, there was an answer.

"Hi. Hi, Grace? Hey. This is Charlie, Althea's friend."

"Hi. Yeah, she mentioned you might call. I got your message the other day, but I've been kind of busy…"

"Listen, are you doing anything right now?"

"Uh—no not until four. Why?"

"Ah—there's this—well, there's this bookstore downtown, Market Street. Have you ever heard of it?"

"The one by the furniture store?"

"Yeah."

"Yeah, yeah I have. But I've never really been in."

"Oh—it's great. It's this old woman's apartment. The first two stories are filled with bookshelves, and everything—even the stove—is stacked with dusty novels, cookbooks, plays, poetry, historical fiction, lawn and garden care, everything. And the woman—she's read like every book in the whole damned place. I go in there and tell her what I've been reading and she throws new authors at me all the time.

Anyway, ah, do you want to go?"

"Sure. Uh—but can you give me a half hour to

get ready?"

"Yeah, sure. I'll pick you up then?"

"Alright. I'll see you—then. Bye."

The road to her house digs deep into the country.

Modest workingmen stoically mow their yards despite the sun. Their crimson skin is hard and somehow heroic in its cover of diffident sweat. One elderly woman wearing a neon orange bathing suit sits in her garden, humming.

To the left are rows of wheat fields waiting for water for life. Their bodies are burned brown by the drought and their limbs hang shallow and gloomy in the earth.

She is standing in the doorway waiting. She is lean and golden, smiling. Grace. I hesitate, and I stammer for the first time in weeks.

"Hey—nice day," I manage, looking backwards. "Um—are you—are you ready?"

She nods yes, a little amused.

Talk about music. A book, a film, a city, an idea. God, man, woman, history, Picasso, Pythagoras, Plato, the view, the allegory of sun cycles. God—anything but the weather. Charm her with your catalogue of colors. Tell her how you watched American movies in Paris. Jazz in Florence. Blues in Chicago. Klinger in Vienna. Pollock in New York.

Anything. Start simple. Talk about life. Begin the first sentence in front of a girl in a long time that isn't designed to seduce or cooperate. Be human, goddammit. Revert to your original form.

The stereo starts with the car, playing Radiohead's Amnesiac.

"Have you heard this yet?"

"Yeah, a little. It came out last week?"

"Yeah."

"I think I like Kid A better. Maybe this one will grow on me, but that record was like—a revelation."

"What else d`you listen to?"

"Nothing really new. A lot of Joni Mitchell, Janis Joplin, Dylan…"

"How the hell does that tie into Radiohead?"

"I don't know——it just all seems like art to me."

Perfect.

The downtown area consists of a few cobblestone roads and row houses, a crumbling single story library, fire department, and a brief block of upscale shops and coffee houses. Off in a corner by itself sits Market Street Books, understated in its width if not by its three-storied height.

The entire face of the first story is cased in glass, and lettered with its logo. This is the best food in town.

Inside we wander separately the rows of dusty bookshelves. The forward front row is packed with novels. All of Balzac, Dickens, Dostoyevsky, Faulkner, Fitzgerald, Hemingway, Hugo, Joyce, Proust, Salinger, and Tolstoy sit waiting for a few dollars to free them home on some eager author, student, or otherwise enthusiast.

I find copies of Rimbaud's *Un Saison Enfer*, and Whitman's *Leaves of Grass* for a friend, and Grace wanders the second row for Drama and Religion.

A few minutes later, I grab Grace and pull her upstairs. Indeed, even the kitchen counters, sink and stovetop are steeped in books.

The second story is a little more contemporary. Here are Burroughs, Bowles, Huxley, Irving, Miller, Morison, and Wolfe.

Grace points to a book with a black spine and red block letters.

"Do you know Anthony Burgess? He wrote A Clockwork Orange…"

"Yeah. Well, I saw the film…"

"Which he hated…" laughing, "anyway I've been reading this." She holds up a paperback copy of The Devil's Mode. "It's a collection of short stories. Have you read Cervantes?"

"Some of Don Quixote…"

"Right. Well, the first story in Devil's Mode has Shakespeare and Cervantes meeting just after the war with Spain and England is ending. But instead of this great meeting between two great writers, the story degenerates into a war over whether the play or the novel is the higher mode of art. Cervantes claims the English plays haven't produced the breadth that a novel is capable of. So Shakespeare counters with a seven-hour play that combines Falstaff and Hamlet. I don't know—I just thought it was great the way they both bickered and fought. I'm sorry, I'm rambling…"

Perfect.

I find a copy of Brave New World to replace the one I'd lent out and never seen again. "Have you read this?"

"I think I—started it—or meant to and never did," laughing. "Is there another copy?" There is. I hand her the better of the two, and hide my long smile behind the bookshelf separating us. What ridiculous joy there is in finding a pretty girl who reads good literature. She pulls out a copy of The Bell Jar and I nearly burst.

Grace starts all of her speeches slowly, becomes swiftly carried away, and eventually ends in a pause and an apology. But you can see the excitement in her eyes, and these speeches become rather endearing rather quickly. She is off topic and unsure, and yet still somehow erudite and graceful.

I am like a moth to a flame.

Back at the house we watch *Dancer in the Dark* on a long L-shaped couch downstairs, covered in blankets and silence. And where other women would ask, "who's that?" or "what happened?" or else call out, "the butler! The butler did it!" Grace just lies there with intent eyes, and muted lips. I have to glance sideways to remind myself she is even there.

Each time I do she smiles hello.

On the car ride home it is as if color is intensified over every shade, hue and tone. Every color creates a contrast with every other color until each object is outlined and personified. And once, where a row of woods would've been background, there is now a livened intensity. It is as if I'm being shaken awake by the only hands that can hold me. And quickly. Ethan's earlier reprimands ring in both ears and echo in my brain.

I watch her linger on the doorstep and drive away.

At night Dean returns with his guitar player and her cousin who is a wine distiller. The three of them steam over gin and tonics and heavy cigars in the hot tub, howling well past 3am.

Upstairs there is much to be done in the way of departing. There are still stacks of bottles to be stowed, floors and counters to be mended, couches to be assembled, drums to be disbanded, and stillness to be restored. I work with plastic bags and antibacterial sprays until spotless shimmering surfaces scream conclusion.

And then the specter reappears.

"Can I come in?"

"If you stay off the floor."

"Dead tonight?"

"Apparently."

"What?"

"Yeah. Yes. I planned it that way though. *They'll* be back tomorrow."

She comes inside and collapses on a nearby couch as if settling herself for the night. "What do you want Lola?"

"A back rub and a hot meal?"

"Not this time."

"Are you trying to avoid me?"

"Is it that obvious?"

"Why?"

"We—you and I—are in the past tense. Over. Fulfilled. Finished. It didn't work out. It was fun, occasionally brilliant, but it burned. It didn't work."

"But why?"

"Jesus—d'you really want me to run through my list of complaints? I don't know Lola. It just stopped moving. It felt frozen, stalled. We were at that point of no return where a commitment becomes concrete and eternal."

"And?"

"Jesus Christ, I'm fucking twenty-two years old! I'm far from finished. I'm beginning. We're both just beginning. There're no reasons to stay with something that's stalled. There're no reasons to stop moving just to store up a little comfort. I'm fucking tired of being comfortable. I want to be challenged. I want movement. I want progress. We—you and I—felt frozen, stopped, stalled. Do you understand?"

"I don't know Charlie. I—I just think you're throwing something great away. You've done this before and—I think you're throwing something away that you'll regret later. I don't know Charlie. I…"

"Enough! Go home. Please. I'm sorry. Go home Lola. I can't. I just can't."

There is nothing more to say. Roll credits and walk down the wooden steps.

The house is quiet now, solemn.

All week you have been alive. Your belly has been filled with dramatic disposition. How does it feel then to have all that vitality stolen? How will you hold up to the static and the silence?

I am no longer afraid of the silence. I am at the beginning in the end, where one story stops and in comes another chasing closely at its heels. Look forward, angel.

chapter seven:

Like Dreaming up from a
Wake.

"Charlie. Hey—it's Grace."

"Hey. Where are you?"

"I'm still at work. I'm sorry—I didn't expect to be here so late. It was sooo busy tonight. I hate my job sometimes."

"That's alright. Do you still want to come over?"

"Umm—yeah. For a little while. I guess I could."

"Are you off yet?"

"Yeah. I want to go home and change though. I'm a mess. So—I'll be there in like—a half hour?"

"Great. There'll be a hot meal waiting."

Laughing, "alright Charlie. I'll see you."

The oven is preheated. I slide a large glass pan inside and set the timer.

The salads are made. The wine is breathing. The bread only needs to be warmed.

The floors are clean. The table is clean. The television has been dusted. A single pillow hangs neatly at each arm of the couch.

And I'm completely insane.

I'm waiting for a girl. Not the queen, or space aliens. I'm waiting for a girl.

Two wine glasses glimmer in the dull candlelight. Plates, bowls, napkins, cutlery. The television has been dusted. Not the queen, or space aliens.

Miles Davis blows gently from beyond the grave.

The door rattles.

"Hey—come in. Have a seat. I just have to get one more thing…"

Grace sits down to a questionably prepared, but lovingly adorned Italian dinner.

"This looks really good. I don't know where to start."

"Yeah. I just hope the taste holds up to the presentation. I…" am going to say something extraordinarily witty right now, at this precise moment in time. "I…umm…do you want to try the bread?"

Her mouth is already full of salad. "In a minute…"

The chicken is relatively tender. The sauce is only a little bitter. Miles Davis blows gently from beyond the grave.

After dinner we sit on the floor in my room and listen to records.

Talk about music. A book, a film, a city, an idea. God, man, woman, history, Picasso, Pythagoras, Plato, the view, the allegory of sun cycles. Anything but the weather.

"So, you're an English major?"

"Yeah."

"What d`you—I mean—who are your favorite authors? You mentioned Burgess before…"

"Yeah—I don't know. I really like William Faulkner."

"Man, what is it about that guy? All my professors were in love with him. Everyone calls him The Great American…."

"You have a problem with *William Faulkner?*"

"I don't know. I mean—I started a few of his books. And I read *Barn Burning* and some of his short stories…but I guess—I just never really related to the characters."

"Oh, but how can you not relate? There's so much there. Everyone's so real. They're all dysfunctional and miserable all the time. I guess the settings are different, and the dialect is…different…but the characters—I mean, they're like family. They're horrible people, but you put up with all of their problems because beneath their inferiorities, there's something—human, something endearing. There has to be, otherwise the story doesn't work."

Upstairs, Grace plays bass.
Her eyes never look up. Her big toe taps a rhythm independent of her foot. Her long hair falls over her shoulders like so much blonde water. I crane my neck slightly from behind a dusty drum set. She doesn't notice. Her eyes never leave her fingers searching frets for the perfect note.

She leaves shortly after on a cigarette. She leaves Joni Mitchell records and creative writing folders. She exhales and drives away before the moment can be spoiled. She always leaves me wanting so much more.
The lamp across the street points out raindrops. They twist and flutter before they hit the ground, catching their share of the air.

···········

To Althea:

Grace is going home on Thursday to attend some sort of family gathering. I'm curious as to (on what level) the other night went over. I think she had a good time. But—god—we get along so well. It's a little frightening. I've seen her three times now, all for around 3-4 hours. And I already know her philosophies on music, movies, college, careers, films, family, people, and cigarettes...

I know her big toe taps out the beat when she plays bass, and that her 2nd toe is longer than her big toe.

I know she's a minister's daughter—and that there is a division between her mother and her—and her father...

I know she really liked the cds I made her—and the salad—and that she thinks my writing needs more dialogue...

I know she was deeply affected by the husband of the professor I was deeply affected by...

I know she's the first girl I've hung out with in ages that I haven't outright tried to sleep with...

I know I don't act in front of her, I 'be'. I'm not used to that.

Anyway—nothing is sealed or sure or secured. I know this. I am under no illusions. But there is a hope again, and I am energized. I am remembering romance. I am awake. And I thank you for the trust, the push, the attachments, and the good taste.

Damnit, I like the girl...

Cheers and confidences—
-charlie.

··········

Grace calls over the weekend. We talk like relative strangers but manage to make plans for the following Tuesday.

··········

On the following Tuesday, I live by the phone. I live by the phone at one o'clock. I sit in bed and watch Saturday Night Live reruns. The phone winks at me as if to tell me what's coming. I tell it to go to hell.

I live by the phone at four. I pick up an old Henry Miller novel for about five minutes before the anticipation becomes too much. I check the phone for a dial tone. I feel like some naïve cheerleader waiting for the fucking quarterback on prom night.

I live by the phone at seven. I sit in bed and watch TV. By now I've had a few.

I live by the phone at ten. I know I should know better. My inner barfly is screaming. I have a few more.

Tim comes home from work after midnight. By now, I have stopped living by the phone. He packs a bowl as I throw the receiver in the backyard.

....

She calls a few days later. I rescue the phone from the recycling bin.

Her voice is shaking. My voice is shaking. Our telephones are hysterical.

"What happened last Tuesday? I thought we had plans. I mean—I waited…"

"Yeah—I did too."

"But you said you'd call me."

"I know. I figured that out halfway through the day. But by then I was too mad to call."

"So we both sat around getting pissed off at each other for not calling?"

"Pretty much."

"That's fucking pathetic!"

"I know! I know. It is."

"Are you alright?"

"I don't know. There's something—I—there's something I wanted to tell you. Charlie, I've been sort of seeing this guy at work—my manager—and—I don't know. I don't really like him. I'm not seeing him anymore. I think.

He won't really leave me alone. God—it's a long fucking story. But—I don't know. I wanted to tell you that. I'm sorry. I suck."

"Yeah. I mean—no. No. It's—it's alright." I don't know whether to laugh or run. "You're not seeing him anymore?"

"No."

"Well——that's fine. I guess. You started seeing him before we met?"

"Yeah."

"Yeah——look, it's no big deal. I can't be offended by something you did before we even met. It's alright. Alright?"

"Yeah. You're awesome Charlie."

"Yeah. You're not so bad yourself sometimes…"

"…"

"Well—why don't you give me a call this weekend?"

"Okay…"

"You call me though, alright? I don't really want to spend another night with my phone. You can't talk to him about a damned thing."

"Yeah. Alright Charlie. Bye…"

··········

There's a pile of dishes in the sink, two stacks of plates on the stove, six glasses, three pots, four bowls, and a graveyard of silverware strewn about the kitchen table.

A thick green film has formed over the liquid left in the pots on the table. Milk is curdled in the glasses. Cigarettes swim in coffee mugs.

Stephen is the center of this mess. Stephen is at work.

I grab a generous pile of plates and pots and, holding them out at arm's length, carry them into his room. I distribute the silverware into several glasses and stack them on the floor next to the plates and pots. I juggle a stack of bowls, spatulas, steak knives, and coffee mugs. I carry them to his room.

I scoop handfuls of rancid rice, beans, hamburger, and cigarette buts out of the drain and toss them into the trashcan. The sink is silver underneath. I never would've guessed silver.

I open the backdoor and let the flies out. A thousand bottles lay dead in large blue containers outside.

I pour the contents of several half-empty cleaning products onto the kitchen table and floor. I throw out the floor mats. I mop, scrub, scour, polish, rinse and repeat. I open curtains, windows, screens, doors, cabinets, anything on a hinge or a wheel. I let all the old air out of the house.

I'm tired of the dust on my bookshelves. I'm tired of the dust in my lungs, bed, eyelids, and motives.

I let all the old air out. I should have done this a long time ago.

Cigarettes and Peaches.

The phone rings near midnight.
"Hey Charlie, it's *me*." She has become a

pronoun.

"Hey Grace. What's up?"

"I'm having some people over. Would you like to be one of them?"

"Yeah. Sure. Who's coming?"

"Cordelia—maybe a few people from work. I don't know…"

"Are we drinking?"

"Yes."

"Should I bring beer or liquor?"

"Umm—liquor?"

"What kind?"

"I don't know. Surprise me."

"Great. I'll see you soon?"

"Yeah. Bye Charlie…"

The drive to Grace's house is only one song long, so I have to choose wisely.

Badly Drawn Boy's Sun Setting begins with a sad string section and a single French horn that bleats in low melodic groans. When the strings fade, a stark acoustic guitar enters, and solemn voice sings:

Now I've fallen in deep,
Slow silent sleep
It's killing me,
I'm dying—
to put a little bit of sunshine in your life.

I could close my eyes right now and nothing would ever matter. Nothing could ever feel as good as this. Hope—

Not the queen, or space aliens.

The porch light is on, and inside I can hear music. I pull up under a tree to the left side of the driveway and walk towards the front door.

"I always know when it's you Charlie. You're the only one who uses that door."

"I just thought it would make a better entrance."

I unload an armful of books, and a bagful of liquor on the kitchen table.

"What's all that?"

"Well—you said you didn't know of any good women authors, so I came bearing Margaret Atwood, Toni Morison, and Carolyn Cassady."

"Thanks." She laughs a little. "Here. You're going to read William Faulkner. Congratulations."

"The Sound and the Fury?"

"Yeah." She bites her lip, lifts her eyebrows, nods, and laughs. "I don't know. Read it. It's good..."

"Damnit."

"Yeah..."

"What are the other two?"

"Glen Gary, Glen Ross is that play I was telling you about. Read it for the dialogue. You'll learn something."

"God, you're vicious!"

"Yeah. Thanks. Uh—the other one I had to read for film class. It's alright I guess. I really don't know why I'm giving it to you."

I look at the cover skeptically. It looks like a fucking western.

"Shane?"

"Aw—come on. It's good. You'll like it."

"I'd better."

I pull up a chair at a little table and begin making makeshift gin and tonics with lime soda.

Sometimes Grace is becoming. Sometimes she is simply stunning. She's not quite classical, but rather, she is the happy mixture of every age strewn together in some sort of post-modern medley. Her face is smooth and long, held up by a lean white neck that reaches into sturdy shoulders. Her lips are ovular and smooth. Her eyes are set back, confident, and gentle. Her over-blonde hair hides rather stylishly behind thin elfin ears.

She doesn't really look like anyone else. Not the queen, or space aliens. Just right.

Grace and I sit on the front porch looking up at the sky. All that's visible are stars and nothingness. Fire and carbon. Diamonds in coal.

Cordelia appears in a rumbling car, parks, exits, and plops down on the grass below us.

"Wow. It's so clear out here."

"I know…"

Cordelia and Grace talk about work. I light a cigarette to keep me company and look at the stars.

From the forest line a little cat creeps up on Cordelia. It pounces on her like a lion and proceeds to purr deeply.

"Do you have a cat?"

"No—but our neighbors have enough for everyone." It looks up at Grace and cranes its overlarge head as if offended.

"Aww—how cute. Go away!"

Inside, Grace washes her hands of kitten allergens and pours herself a glass of peach snaps and sprite. Next she shows off a crocheted cap colored six ways in star patterns as Cordelia bounces a rubber ball dully on the floor. Cordelia is kind and easy to talk to, if not a little mordant.

"Sarcasm—that's my name!" She spouts happily.

A Joni Mitchell record spins in the background. Her voice and soft-strummed melodies contain all the restrained virtue of an ailing mother singing apolitical lullabies to her child. I stand crouched in the hallway listening to River.

It's coming on Christmas,
they're cutting down trees
and putting up reindeer…
I wish I had a river I could skate away on…

An hour later Cordelia's little car rumbles away, and Grace and I linger outside on a couple of smokes.
"Do you want to sit on the car—you know—to keep away from the cat? I think I can improvise a blanket."
(Laughing) "Sure."
I put a black turtleneck over the layer of midnight mist on top. Grace stumbles a little on the slick edges, before seeing my hand and happily obliging.

The shallow width of the car causes us to lean into each other, and it becomes quickly clear that this is where I have to make a move.

God, man, woman, history, Picasso, Pythagoras, Plato,
the view…
Not the queen, or space aliens…

Without warning the little cat leaps up onto the hood and prances quickly toward us with wide eyes and a humming belly.

"Damnit cat…" Grace laughs. She is tender to it despite her reactions to its fur. I hold its tail off her nose and pull it my way. It curls up into a ball and rumbles.

A low hanging branch grazes the top of the car just behind us. I see cigarettes fading and become concerned. Conversation has stalled. The silence is like a noose around us.

Even Grace's eyes have become quizzical. I can tell she is about to give up.

"Do you want to go inside?"

"…" "Okay."

The kitten frowns. The girl moves left off of the car.

But somehow my arm slides around her waist and pulls her back. I pull her towards me, lean in and dissolve, like sugar into an ocean.

I slide my free hand behind her head, and we fall into the car. The thin metal gives a little and forms a crater. I kiss her all the way to the bottom.

Time passes around us like sped up stock footage, like hours of clouds racing into a storm, or a science film blooming roses. I kiss her all the way to the bottom.

She tastes like peace schnapps. Her fingers roam my shoulders lightly.

I explore the base of her neck and move upwards to her earlobe. I hear her breath against my in turned ear.

I look up to see her face. Her mouth stays slightly open and the edges of her lips curl upwards into a smile a decade long.

Sonic Youth and Joni Mitchell clash through open windows.

Eventually, we make it inside, holding on to each other unsteadily up the redbrick steps and stumbling through her incessantly sticking front door.

We sit on syndicated chairs in the living room and watch television as fingers find fingers, and kisses are stolen over commercial breaks.

And I hold her in the doorway. And I go home in new skin.

The roof of the car pops out in a loud clap as I shut the door.

....

The phone rings earlier the next night.
"Hi." We are beyond pronouns.
"Hi."
"So—are you coming over?"

What is my stomach doing? It doesn't want food. It doesn't really want to talk or sing or dance. It just wants to spin.

Oh right—

I meet Grace at the door. We say nothing.

I walk through without touching her. But inside, I lean over and remind myself on her lips.

She still tastes like peaches.

Shortly after, three cars pull up and produce people. Grace invites them in, seats them at mismatched chairs around the kitchen table, and distributes beer.

Cordelia and Grace talk about work.
"Have you met Henry yet? The cook?"
"I think so…"
"The other night that fucker smeared mayonnaise on my shirt. So I threw a glass at his head and he thought I was *flirting*…"
"What?"
"I know!"

Jermaine, tall and highly animated, joins in.
"Look at these shoes!" He holds them up to expose their worn underbelly. "They're great. I can slide all the way across the kitchen on mop water."
"Didn't you knock off a pile of plates on the prep table doing that?"
"Yes! Damnit—" rolling up a pant leg. "I have scars…"

Grace produces two coffee mugs and calls quarters. Her and Jermaine toast coins and quickly sink shots into upright coffee cups. Pass left. Fail and sink and pass left. Catch up and stack and spin the coin. Cordelia catches one under her finger with a wide grin. A full beer disappears.
I falter early but recover. Grace drinks. Then Jermaine three times. Then I, twice. Then Jermaine once. Then Grace again. Then she hits the rebuttal and I drink twice more. The laughter and applause gets louder and drunker each time.
The guy in the corner without a name never touches his glass.
Cordelia and Grace talk about work.

I can't talk here. I haven't slid on mop water. I don't know anything about being molested by the cook, and I haven't been in a decent food fight for ages. I quit my job months ago, and haven't had a sufficient story since.

Why do people find it necessary to talk about mop water?

We carry on with the game until our stomachs are swollen, the refrigerator is vacated, and Grace's poor counter is covered in empty green bottles. The others move into the yard for stars and cigarettes. I catch Grace behind the door and remind myself.

Soon, everyone's gone home. Grace and I stand in the kitchen for a minute admiring the mess. Then we start shedding cotton onto the kitchen floor. She is pale and slender underneath.

I don't know why I do a lot of things.

The drinks are hitting me. The world is shaking and her body is beating against me like a tide.

We move into the bedroom. Her legs are eight miles long. I'm tangled up. My head is spinning from the booze.

Grace pulls away, apologizes, and goes to the bathroom.

Michael Stipe is singing about water and streetlights. I drift off.

When she comes back, the sun's coming up behind us, and we've nothing left to hide under.

She slithers back into position, but by now neither of us have the energy to make love or war. We slide together quietly for a little while before it's painfully clear we're both too tired. I roll sideways and wrap around her. And there's silence for sometime after.

"Charlie?"

"Yeah?"

"Do you want to have a cigarette?"

"Outside?"

"Yes."

Grace puts on a faded pink bathrobe, and I, a pair of pants. Outside, I put an arm around her as she leans into my shoulder.

"Charlie?"

"Yeah?"

"I don't know. I feel…I feel oddly domestic."

"Yeah."

The sun has risen.

Inside, I get a glass of water and lean out the kitchen window overlooking the orange cornfield in her back yard.

And I realize how much I've misread everything. I realize the great gift of starting over.

· · · · · · · · · ·

When I wake up, the bedroom is empty and the house is still. I get dressed and have a look.

Grace is sitting in the center of the living room in silence.

"Hi."

"Hi."

"You're leaving again today?"

"Yes."

"How long this time?"

She turns toward me. I see for the first time

that green light that Gatsby must have seen. I see why he made his millions just so he could throw her those ridiculous parties. I see why he caught so many moths looking for a single butterfly.

"Week and a half."

My mouth is dry. My tongue tastes like so much stale beer.

"Hey—do you have an extra toothbrush?"

"No."

"Would you mind terribly if I borrowed yours for a second?"

"Yes!"

"Ok—never mind. Sorry"

I kiss her anyway, and am somewhat surprised at how tenderly I am received. Her eyes are tender too.

I leave in that look. I drive down deserted highways wondering what will happen in a week and a half.

chapter eight:

Time and Distance

To Grace:

Delia and Althea drove down to see Stephen last night. I forgot that Delia's staying with you during the semester. It's strange, after everything, to think of that place as anyone else's.

Anyway, we drank jug wine out of your Ikea glasses, and I fried some chicken in olive oil and breadcrumbs, and added a bag of stir-fry and a box of rice.

And walking around, I felt like I had filmed a movie there. I felt like I was hanging out on the set where once some story had come alive in a flash of lights, cameras, gaffers, boom mikes and light poles. After the film, it's hard to look at the set without seeing through the eyes of its actors.

It's funny—I've been having problems with Stephen all summer. Ever since Althea left he's been a field for evil, and lately, he's been getting even worse. But he's a completely different person when she's here. With her, there is no evil. There is wild—but there is compassion as well. I forgot that fucker got like that.

So you have excellent friends. They improve without weighing on your freedom.

And I liked your kitchen. There's enough room in there to cook abstractly. I'd like to cook you dinner again when you get back. I know you hate plans—but I'm not nearly as worried as I was about finding time between your twenty jobs, friends, and hermit instincts. I'll fit in somewhere. I'd like to.

I meant what I said about feeling honest around you. It seems like it's been a while. For the longest time I felt like I was like sleeping through my own conversations. I don't feel like that now. I feel like I'm picking things up where previously I had been on pause. I feel like I've made the shift and now the music makes sense, and the writing falls out like rain. I feel like I've shifted my instincts.

Now there's a girl that doesn't care so much about family money, or writerdom, or musiciandom, or any other iconic fallacies, so much as she does about being treated well, and connecting.

Anyway, I just wanted to let you know that I had fun those last two nights. And I'm having fun here and hope you are there. I hope your father lives up to his potential "coolness." I hope your sister is coming out of that odd phase of false middle-adolescent values. I hope Ikea shines as always.

I hope to see you when you get back.

-charlie

Oddly Domestic.

Tim wanders the front yard with a cigarette while I stare down my favorite streetlight. It seems like I've spent most of my life on porches, waiting to go somewhere.

"I don't know man. This is all so strange. Everything's strange. After everything with Lola and Eve, I figured I'd have to be alone for a while. I'd known both of them so long, I d invested so much in the past—I never thought I'd find anything resembling a present or a future so easily—so quickly. This is all so strange. It's like some beautiful dream."

Tim flicks his cigarette into the bushes and looks up. "You're awake Charlie."

....

She shows up after midnight, thin and quiet.
"So—how was the trip?"
"Alright, I guess. My dad wasn't really there,

which is always good. I don't know. As much as I hate this town, it's always nice to get back."

Stephen and his new girl are curled up on the couch watching *Crocodile Hunter*.

"Oh—I love this guy!"

"Yeah, me too. This `ere is the most dangerous animal in the entire world. I'm gowin to pick `im up and twirl `im round me head!"

The four of us smoke cigarettes on the front porch. Stephen is laughing his ridiculous laugh. He sounds like a cartoon villain.

Grace and I walk into the yard to see the stars. My hand makes small circles on her back. She leans in.

Stephen and the girl laugh in the background. But nothing matters anymore. She has kissed me in public.

Inside, we consume more beer and television. I'd like to be entertaining. I'd like to stroll into a jazz club and order a pair of gin and tonics. I'd like to roll around on a shoreline somewhere. I'd like the sounds of current clashing with sand, and the way the salt floats on air. I'd like to take her to a fair, like every asshole in every bad date movie. I'd win her the forty foot purple elephant and buy her armfuls of balloons and spun sugar, and then we'd look down from the Ferris wheel and comment on how all the people look like ants.

Then we'd chase each other through the fun house. Then we'd sail away on swans.

I wonder why nobody does any of that here. That's how people act in movies, but in real life, all we really do is sit around a television like ancient civilizations must have sat around fires or statues. In real life, there's never a girl and a carnival in the same week.

In real life we tend to complain before aspire.

Grace cranes her neck backwards to see the clock.

"Jesus! It's four in the morning! I've really gotta go Charlie."

"Look—it's late. You're pretty far from sober, why don't you stay here?"

"I can't. I've gotta work in the morning, and I haven't been home all week. And I was really looking forward to sleeping in my own bed again."

"You sure you're alright to drive?"

"No, but I've done it before. I'll be alright."

I say goodbye and light up a smoke. Stephen is already on the porch counting his own ashes.

"What happened to Grace?"

"She went home—said she had to work in the morning."

"Man—after the show you two put on out here? That sucks. I was sure you were gonna score."

"Yeah, thanks…"

Inside, a little red light flashes by the phone in the living room. It's Grace's number.

I call back. The rings hang hard in the empty air. Nothing. I missed her by five minutes.

"Damnit!"

....

The phone rings earlier the next night.

"Hi."

"Hi."

"So—are you coming over?"

Am I moving backwards?

There's a long column of cars in the driveway. I park off to the side so as to distinguish myself, and go in through the back door.

Inside, Cordelia and Grace talk about work. A young man, twenty, with short black hair, stretched skin, and a long face sits between them giggling girlishly.

"Charlie, you know Jack, don't you?"

"No. It's ahh—it's nice to meet to you. Do you all work at..."

"Yeah, yeah. Nice to meet you—Hey Gracy, were you there the other day when we ran out of onions?"

I grab a beer and try not to furl my eyebrows too much. Sometimes I feel like Charlie Brown listening to his teachers talk. I nod when someone makes eye contact, and I laugh when their voices go up at the end of a long sentence. But that's the best I can do.

Every now and then Grace eyes me apologetically.

At one Jack is talking badly about his managers. Grace and Cordelia laugh along.

At two Jack is talking badly about the dishwashers. Grace and Cordelia yawn and laugh along.

At three Jack is talking badly about the customers. Cordelia yawns politely and drives away. Grace laughs occasionally.

At four, Grace begins stretching obviously and rolling her eyes at me under the table. Jack's own eyes are popping out of their sockets. He seems so excited to be able to hear himself talk. He's the entertainment and the audience. He tells the stories and then reacts to them.

His skin gets tighter each hour. I'm starting to be able to visibly see the currents of blood coursing through his forehead. He'd be downright menacing if he weren't so fucking feminine. He's like a non-threatening mugger. He catches people in alleyways and talks them into submission.

"Give me your money, or I'll talk about the casualties of mop water!"

"Take it! Take it—Christ! Shut up! Shut up! Shut up!"

I kick over the table and break my chair on his back. Grace gags him with a placemat and binds his arms with the tablecloth. His eyes bulge like an insect's. His veins pulse in Morse code:

.-- ..-. . / -.-- --- ..- / - .... . .-. . / - .... . / --- - .... . .-. / -.. .- -.-- / .-- .... . -.

Grace looks at me curiously.

"Oh—nothing. Sorry I—drifted off."

"Yeah, I'm getting tired too."

Jack continues to talk. I'm getting the feeling he's trying to outlast me—as if the last man here automatically gets the girl. I blink at him:

--. --- / - .... . / ..-. ..- -.-. -.- / .... --- -- .
--. --- / - .... . / ..-. ..- -.-. -.- / .... --- -- .
--. --- / - .... . / ..-. ..- -.-. -.- / .... --- -- .

At five Jack is on the doorstep saying goodbye. I hold up my trophy and gloat at the back of his head. Grace is busy hiding in the bathroom.

"It's over now, honey. He's gone. That man can't hurt us anymore."

"God—I didn't know what to say. I tried yawning every thirty seconds but he didn't even flinch."

"I don't think he's human. Did you see the veins in his forehead?"

"I try not to look directly at them."

"Yeah——man, you look like hell."

"Yeah, thanks."

"Do you want me to get out of here?"

"Yeah. I'm sorry, it's just sooo late. Come on, I'll walk you out."

I kiss her in the driveway. She lets go. I grab her again. I let go. She grabs me again.

The sun is coming up behind us.

It Rings to Tell You What the Future Holds.

"Hey Charlie."

"Hey Grace. What's up?"

"Not much. I've been lying in bed all day, and I kind of feel like getting out of the out house."

"You've been in bed all day? But it's like— eight o'clock..."

"Yeah, I know. But Star Wars was on this morning, so I had to watch that. And then Oprah was on...I guess everything sort of went downhill from there..."

"Jesus. Yeah. Well—there's a couple people over here. We're just having a few beers and talking about Vedantic Meditation."

"Ahh—Henry's there. Yeah, I'll be there in a

little while. I've still got to get a shower."

"Alright. I'll see you soon."

Tim, Stephen, Sid, Henry, and James Watson pass a tube of smoke around the living room.

"Who was that Fell?"

"Grace. She'll be by in a little while. She has to take a shower."

"At eight o'clock?"

"Yeah—well—Oprah was on…"

Jude exhales and coughs his eyes into a crimson stream.

"Is that the girl you've been talking about?"

"Yeah, that's her."

Tim exhales, "you want some?"

I don't know why I do a lot of things.

An hour later things start spinning. The lines in the fake wood flap like curtains by an open window.

Everyone goes out on the porch for cigarettes. I go to the kitchen for a glass of water.

Grace appears in the living room. Just like that.

I kiss her hello. My hands find that happy curve on her hips. Her lips arch up in a smile.

Then she backs away.

"Charlie—your friends are a little strange."

"Oh yeah? What'd they want?"

"I don't know. That guy with the glasses…"

"James?"

"I guess. He kept telling me how much he'd heard about me, and that he's seen my picture…"

"Yeah, I have shrine built in the backyard, d'you wanna see it?"

"Not really."

"Well—do you want a beer?"
"I think I'd better…"

The crowd comes in and continues to smoke. Grace has a few to catch up while I watch the walls wave. Soon we're all out of focus.

I can feel my heart beating and it bothers me a little. I scratch around awkwardly for Grace's hand. Her lips arch up in a smile, but her eyes are hardly open anymore.

Talk about music. A book, a film, a city, an idea.

The walls are waving at me. James's glasses make his eyes seem even more microscopic. I can hear the hum of the television. I can make out Tim's laugh. It's in a higher key but it manages to maintain a lower tone. It's the perfectly equalized laugh.

I fumble to put my arm around Grace. We smile at each other politely.
"D`you want—uh`nuther beer?"
"No—I'm awkay…"

At three Grace is yawning. The room has emptied, and I'm starting to come down.
"Do you want to go in my room?"
"Yeah. Okay…"
I turn on the television and pull back the sheets. Grace collapses.
I curl in and kiss her. Her lips barely part.
"I'm sorry. I'm just really tired…"
"That's alright. Close your eyes. I just— wanted to say goodnight.
"Goodnight Charlie."

The television goes black. All I ever really wanted was a girl there when the television goes black. I close my eyes

Ten minutes later she rolls over.
"I'm sorry. I just—I feel a little uncomfortable being here. I don't know..."
"Yeah? Is there's anything—I can do? I mean—I want you to be comfortable here. I want you to feel—safe…"
"I know. I don't know what it is. I'm sorry."
"That's alright———I'm glad you came..."
"So am I..."

We're quiet on the sidewalk, saying goodnight a second time.

....

The bed is curiously bare in the morning. I feel like a small child waking up in a large open field of amber wheat.

My head hurts a little. But at least the walls are still. At least I can focus on that.

It feels like tiny cracks and fissures are opening up. Lately, Grace and I have spent all our time together dumbfounded and drunk amid odd crowds. I wonder if a night of sobriety would distill some of the distance. I'd like to regain the ground I grew in bookstores, and over intelligible conversations, movies, home cooked meals, and decade smiles.

Sometimes I'm halfway convinced that she's going to destroy me, or that she's secretly the fully imagined remnants of my inner child.

All we have now are stolen kisses in secret

kitchen corners. That's lovely. But we could be so much more than two hermits dancing around each other in equally odd social situations.

I know she likes homemade things. I remember the candleholder she made out of "clothesline wire," the hat she crocheted, the sculptures, paintings, watercolors, and photographs.
I know she's working tonight.

I get in my car and drive towards one of those corner gas stations that sells cheap individually wrapped roses out of large spherical Gatorade containers. No luck.

I try another with the same result. I try a grocery store with a small floral section near the vegetable isle. The clerks stare at me in my crumbling black and white Chuck Taylors and wild-eyed determined t-shirt and black pants slouch. They're sold out. I try another. It's 6:30 and all the flower shops are closed. I drive ten miles down the road, five miles back, six miles left, and 300 yards backwards. I find the last bitter individually wrapped single red rose on the face of the planet. I hold it up in defiance of God.

I write her a letter. I write her a *real*, scribbled mad, honest, impossibly poetic, *here's how the fuck I feel and here's what I'm willing to do about it* letter.

I leave it on her doorstep along with the last flower nature ever bore. I can still hear it in the back of my mind, pleading:

I can't say I'm not rattled, or that I haven't been thinking about the causes of our recent rigidity, or that I don't feel it as well.

Sometimes you seem so breakable underneath everything. I try so hard not to invade your space, or crack your shell. I sit quietly in crowds to just to prove how well I fit and how little I intrude.

I really like you—and at the same time, I'm terrified of you. You're a girl unlike any other I've come across, and I must say that I'm a little intimidated by equals. Half the time, I'm waiting for someone to run out into the street with an armful my writing, screaming "bullshit!" The other half, I'm hiding from the weight of being a creator, as if the first failure would negate all the years of progress and condemn me to a life of normalcy among the factories my father frequented after Vietnam traded him his inner child for a lifetime supply of vodka and demons.

You have adult eyes and the heart of a child. You are aware of danger, and yet not so free-spirited as to jump into a fire simply for the heat. You understand that just because something shines, doesn't mean it can't burn you as well. You're like me.

I'm not sure what you want—or that you even know either. But you do seem willing to try. And I'm at least grateful for that.

Half the time I feel like I don't deserve any of this, so I hide in bottles and guitars. I hide in the awkward moments that keep you safe from success. Success is, after all, the single most frightening prospect to people like you and I. We were raised in contradictions. Your mother and father are contradictions. Your father is a walking contradiction.

Sometimes I feel like I stumbled into everything worthwhile. I guess I just have to realize that you're here for a reason, that you've put up with your own doubts, and the odd timing and awkward air that lives between us. You're still here. So far, at least…

It's just—for one moment last night I realized that you were here—and that I didn't have to do anything. And it was so peaceful.

But last night was built on eggshells. It's strange having

you around friends. Every other girl I've ever brought around them has either sat silent and sullen and guarded, or else jumped into their arms and twirled locks of plastic hair and battered eyelashes.

And maybe you're not completely comfortable—but you never once seemed resentful, or jealous, or threatened. Maybe I have to get used to that. Maybe I have as much guard to let down as you do. Maybe you fit too easily, or too well. It's like walking into the sun after spending all my days in dark rooms. Light doesn't always make sense. You want go back inside and sleep.

Feel free to throw this fucking thing away at any time. I just wanted to apologize for all the awkwardness. I don't know if this will do away with any of that—but it was worth a try. It's just—the accumulated effect of GRACE is something great and beautiful—worth words better than that. And as someone who speaks often on the behalf of beauty, thanks for existing. Thank you for putting up with rambling poets. We mean well, I swear. We're just not very good at normalcy. And maybe that's it after all. Lately, you and I have tried to exist in normal situations, and I always think we should be on Saturn. Imagine the beautiful girl who lies in bed hiding all day, over Oprah, Chewbacca, and clay sculptures meeting Dostoyevsky's Underground Man and going to a party. No wonder things got weird.

…and I meant to tell you—as if this makes any sense, or really relates to anything other than the fact that I am rambling. But things pop up in your head over the course of the evening. I meant to tell you kiss like water. You bend back and drift—become fluid and smooth. Kissing you is sort of like swimming. It's nice.

Anyway—

It's noon on a Thursday. I'm half awake and laughing at myself. But I feel better. Writing always helps me figure things out. Hopefully, this'll shed some light on you as well.

*So—I wrote this a few hours ago. It's a little
oversimplified, but I think it's a good way to end:*

*Take time,
To sleep off the generations of confusion
And forgive the boy who promised poetry
And produced only endless hours of television—*

*Forgive the past that never saw
That a little space was all you needed—*

Or that a tree shakes better than a television—

Or that homemade beats moneymade—

That thought is preferable to mass production—

That a girl is as breakable as a boy—

I'll admit I don't know you as much as I'd like to—

*I do notice the differences in crowds,
And how secretive you are of yourself*

*I notice the silence you seek
Being stolen away by poor motives
"Make my bed—" says a stranger
"Hold my dreams," says another
I know you only want to hold your own.
I know how delicately dreams are held.*

*I know you come from another planet
Where quiet is comfort is dedication,
Where simplicity is righteous,
Where we make ourselves out of clay*

If only for the joy of creation
Where satisfaction is alone, is comfort,
Where comfort is perceived in strokes of silence,
Where silence is received in satisfaction—

And maybe once you were outside,
And the light was crooked,
And the air of silence was stolen,

And maybe you were forced into things
With jagged edges that never quite fit right.

And maybe nothing ever fit right,
Maybe you always felt your shape bending—

But I'll promise at the beginning
Of whatever is or isn't to be
That I'll never steal your shape,
That I'll never steal the silence,
Or bend the dreamer

I like the color and the shape.
I like the eyes and the insides,
The smooth skin and estranged spirit
That makes you appreciate awkward dialogue
As human truth

And I'll be here whenever you feel like coming out of that cave
And I swear there's honestly more here than television and indoor
games,

And maybe I'm afraid to fall as well
And maybe I have my own ghosts and effigies of the past

But I don't believe in circles anymore,
I've run around in still shades so long.

I'm ready for growth,
However slow or delicate—

I'm ready to try
Whenever you are—

Be well.
Know there's someone close that understands confusion,
And that he'll never hammer out the edges,
And that he only wants to ease
What the world called progress—

Know there's someone close, who wants to hold the dreamer,
But doesn't want to shift the dream.

Sleep sound and safely
Know I'll be there
Whenever you feel like being awake again.

-charlie

chapter nine:

The Deafening Indifference.

Tim and I stand out on the porch smoking when a large black man on an old green bicycle stops and calls out from the street.

"Yo!"

"Ah—yeah?"

"You the one that's got a drum set?"

"Yeah."

"I heard you a little while ago. I was just next door. You're not bad."

"Thanks."

"You know, I play too."

"Yeah? What's your name?"

"Lamont."

"I'm Charlie. This is Tim. Hey, d'you want to come in and check out the set?"

"Hell yeah."

Lamont looks to be in his late twenties. He's heavy—but he's tall too. When he sits down at the kit he looks like he's sitting down on something built for a small child.

The attic is oppressively hot. I flick on one of the amps and plug in a guitar. Lamont starts off the beat and fumbles for a few minutes. But eventually, he gets his rhythm and sticks some great backbeats on my wandering guitar licks.

Tim sits on the couch at the other end of the attic and nods his head. I can see his eyes start to turn upward at what's coming together.

When I play faster, Lamont bears down harder on the toms and kicks up the beat into fury of sawdust and sweat. The sweat starts streaming down from my forehead too, and it burns my eyes mercilessly. But I only play through it, strumming as hard as I can, breaking through the pain with shear volume and speed, kicking and leaping into the air as a cymbal finally crashes a release.

Lamont lays down his sticks and sighs.

"Man—that was some serious shit we just played."

"I know. You're pretty damned good back there. It took you a minute, but…"

"I got the hang of it."

"You sure as hell did."

"Man—I gotta split. Is it alright if I holla at you guys later?"

"Any time man."

"Cool. I'll be around."

Ephemera.

I haven't heard from Grace in a few days. I am the patron saint of jumping to conclusions.

The phone rings a little after five o'clock. The voice on the other end tells me my first novel has just been released. I thank it and hang up.

Did I mention I was a writer?

I don't know. I don't understand. I don't understand anything anymore.

It's evening again. It's near autumn and the leaves look golden in the twilight.

Sometimes I wish I hadn't the problems of a man, where waking incites actions certain to become memory; where memories are sure to mix the blessings and the nightmares; where nightmares tend to appear during the day once properly ignored; where intelligence denounces ignorance and makes then it's own form of ignorance—grand and grave and impossible to shake.

O, I wish I had the problems of a tree that swayed—swayed on a stiff, but welcome spring rain that comes to shake the life awake after a long winter. Alas, I am a man.

I'm looking up. I'm looking at that streetlight that should be green and across the bay. And it's the most desolate thing I've ever seen.

What the fuck is wrong with me?

....

The phone rings.

"Charlie?"

"Yeah?"

"Hey—it's Grace."

"Hey Grace. How've you been?"

"I've been getting ready for this trip. I told you about that right? God, I've been sooo busy…"

"You're going to Canada this time?"

"Yeah. Yeah, I'm going for three weeks as a counselor for all the freshmen. Oh, it's going to be great."

"When are you leaving?"

"Sunday."

"Can I see you this weekend?"

"Umm—I don't think I really have any time. I'm sorry. We're having a meeting tonight with all the counselors, and tomorrow we're meeting with all the kids. I haven't even had a chance to pack."

"Yeah. Well—you'd better get started."

"Yeah…"

"Hey—maybe I'll talk to you when you get back. Have a good trip Gracy."

"Yeah, alright. Charlie?"
"Yeah?"
"Take care alright?"
"Yeah."

The dial tone is like a death rattle.

I fall over. I hit a wall. I hit a wall with my
heart, and then with my fist. I put a hole in Jack
Kerouac's left knee.

*TTTHHHHHWWWWAAAKAKAKAKAKA
KAKAKAKAAAAAHHHHHH!*

Letters never mean a thing.
God, I need a drink. I need two liters of
whiskey all at once. I need to feel each drop screaming
down, melting my liver, boiling in my stomach. I want
the half hour of numbness before the sickness hits.
Maybe I'll even skip the sickness. Maybe I'll go farther.
I poured my pathetic little heart out. Now it feels like
it's getting too big for my chest. I think I can actually
feel it trying to liberate itself from this sorry body.
The white rim around the hallway is the gate to heaven.
I'm on the floor looking through it. Why can't I be
there and not here? Why can't there be peace? Peace!

*TTTHHHHHWWWWAAAKAKAKAKAKA
KAKAKAKAAAAAHHHHHH!*

Nothing.

I stand up and look at the room. The spinning
has stopped.
I reach for the phone.

"Grace?"

"Yeah?"

"Hi. I'm sorry, but can we talk for five minutes like we know each other?"

"Yeah—I'm sorry. I know…"

"This is ridiculous…"

"I know…"

"We're two intelligent people blessed with large vocabularies and eloquent tongues about the English language—and yet we can't communicate a single fucking thing to each other."

"I know."

"I wrote you a letter the other day. I left it on your doorstep."

"I know. I got it."

"Yeah?"

"Yeah—it was beautifully written. But I don't know how much I can trust your writing. It's so good sometimes that I think you could talk anyone into anything."

"I meant every word."

"I don't know Charlie. You might have. But it seemed like you were just trying to write a really great letter when—maybe you should've just tried to write a really honest letter."

"I meant every word."

"Yeah. Well, it was a really *great* letter. I just— there's so much going on right now, and…"

"And I'm only asking for a small part of that."

"Yeah, but I know how *I* am. It's not so easy for me to play a small part. Once I get into something, I always try to make it work, and—I just can't do that right now."

"Look—I'm going to be busy too. The book just came out…"

"Hey, congratulations!"

"Yeah, thanks. But I've got that to deal with, and school's starting in a few weeks…"

"As soon as I get back."

"Yeah. I know. The point is, I'm not going to have a whole lot of time either. But I know I'd rather spend what little time is left with you than on the television or the bar or the street. I'm not asking a lot Grace. I don't know—I get the impression that I make you happy."

"You do, Charlie…"

"Well, that's all I'm asking for. I don't want to intrude on your productivity. But I'd love to have the chance to fill in those small spaces in between."

"I really have to go now."

"Yeah…"

"I'll call you when I get back, alright?"

"Yeah."

"Charlie?"

"Yes?"

"Thank you."

··········

Tim comes home from work an hour later. I tell him every hard detail and we decide to take it out on a local bar.

Henry's band is loading equipment through the back door. We grab guitar cases and stroll in with them to avoid the cover.

Just inside the door is a pool table where six girls, Grace and five others, are standing around nursing little plastic glasses of coke and water. Tim gasps a little under his breath, and I choke on mine.

Grace walks over.

"Hey—I thought you might be here."

"Oh yeah? Why'd you think that?"

"Well, all your friends are *right* over there…"

Sure enough, Sid, Jude, James Watson, and several others are sitting up at the bar surrounded by empty bottles.

"I'll be right back…"

I walk up to the crowd as an excuse to catch my breath. They all dumbly announce my name into the smoky, stale bar air. James corners me.

"Hey Charlie! Did you see Grace?"

"Yeah, I just said hello. Did you talk to her?"

"Only for a second. I said, *'Hey you're Charlie's girl aren't you?'* or something like that. I'm kind of hammered, if you couldn't tell…"

"What did she say?"

"She said—I don't know, man…"

"Come one, this is important…"

"She said, *'Yes—I suppose I am.'*"

"Really?"

"Yeah. Really. Hey, who are those girls she's with?"

"I couldn't tell you…"

'Yes—I suppose I am.' Man, that sounds damned good. I tell Tim.

"That's a good sign right?"

"Yeah. You should go talk to her. And who are those other girls?"

"I don't know," I start laughing. "But come on, I'll introduce you."

Grace and the girls move to a table opposite the bar.

"What are you guys doing here?"

"We just wanted to play a game of pool before the meeting tonight. But those assholes in the yellow shirts are trying to kick us out."

"Why?"

"We're all underage."

"Oh, yeah. Well—you just wanted to play one game?"

"Yeah..."

"Hold on."

There's an empty table in the far corner. Tim secures it along with a handful of beers. I go back for the girls.

Five minutes later, we're well into a game of doubles. Tim misses a shot, but corners a little blonde girl. I accidentally make one and pass out Marlboros. Then one of the yellow shirts strolls over to free us of our women. I tell it they're with us and will leave after the game is through. It huffs, but agrees.

Tim and I start throwing shots to save the scenery.

After the game, I walk Grace and the girls outside. She's a stark contrast to her friends. They all giggle and whisper whenever we're close. They're nice kids, but they belong in a mall or at a keg party. They act like little girls away from home for the first time. Like Lola was. They're unfinished.

There's nothing missing in Grace. She belongs in a painting or a song or on Saturn. Grace is a woman.

This is the first time I've really noticed.

She leans in slowly. Like sugar into an ocean. All the way to the bottom. Like sped up stock footage. Hours of clouds. A science film blooming roses. Cigarettes and peaches. All the way to the bottom.

· · · · · · · · · ·

One thing I miss in all this summer stoicism—
through all the hazy afternoons, when warped concrete
shakes in the still, humid air, and the sky is stiff and
sunny and blue—

O, how I miss those winter nights when the
snow starts falling against that blanket of black. And
how like wishes are snowflakes, falling on a swing from
left to right, thinking about that moment just past when
they were born and first saw the world. How beautiful
it must be to be born in the air and see the world in
slow motion all the way into the ground. How much
hope there is in a snowflake falling.

And somewhere there's a little fire. And a little
lock of grey dust is sailing up from the flames, and a
puff of white ice is drifting down. And the ash and
snow meet halfway and dance. And the fire cackles
with soft laughter. And the smell is at once crisp and
heavy. How close am I now to dancing in the snow—

How Grace would look at me and laugh. How
her cheeks would glow like a fireplace. How that smile
that's too big to be true would look on a crimson leash.
How I can tell when she's smiling even with my head
buried in streaks of her hair.

chapter ten:

I n t e r m i s s i o n .

Lamont and I are driving around town. The sun has long since sunken below the silver oil towers and little one story yellow houses with white shudders. He's at the wheel blasting the latest hip hop group.

"Did I ever tell you that I know a girl who knows a girl who messed around with Pink?"

"Was he black?"

"Yep."

"I knew it! I knew it! I knew it!" Lamont starts pumping his fist and screaming, "woo! Yes! I knew it! Yes!"

For five minutes he's rocking the car back and forth and shouting. I feel people drive by and wonder if he's having a seizure.

"I told my girl. I told her Pink messes around with black dudes."

"There you…"

"Fuck yeah! Woo! Woo!"

The streets are blank and undecipherable from one to the next. We drive onward, not knowing where we're going.

Lamont takes up half the car. He's probably 6'5" and nearing 300 lbs, but he drives with a relaxed sort of jerk.

His seat's reclined like a roadster in a rap video. Every now and then he takes a sniff from a little metal tube and scratches at his nose.

Despite all this—he really is one of the nicest, most genuine people I've ever met. He's the sort of guy who would lay down in traffic for you. And I'd probably do it for him. Not only do you rarely meet *people* like that—but it's almost as important to all of us that he's a black man in a black neighborhood who's always done nothing but embrace our household that has been painfully white. Beside the friendship, he's showed our neighbors that we aren't prejudiced against anyone who treats us with respect.

When he's finished scratching his nose, Lamont starts drifting off on something out the window. "So—what happened with that job?"

"Man—I don't know. They hired me—right—and now they're trying to say it was pending a background check."

"Well, did you list everything on the application?"

"Yeah. Damn right. They asked if I ever committed a felony, and I wrote *yes* and explained what happened."

"That's pretty fucked up."

"Tell me about it."

"So what's your record look like?"

"Man—I've got a gun charge, an assault charge, a drug charge, and a child abuse charge."

"Damn."

"Yeah—well the child abuse charge is kind of fucked up."

"How so?"

"Man—I hit my kid once. I was reprimanding him and I hit him. You know? That's the way I grew up. That's how my pops kept me in line, so that's what I know to do…"

"Right…"

"But then the next day, the babysitter saw some marks on his thigh and called child services."

"Shit"

"But man—check it out. That was the same week that some mother got convicted of beating her kid to death, and they were trying to make examples of people. It hit my kid *one* time—that's it—and they send me to jail for that."

"What about the weapons and drugs?"

"Ah—I got caught with a little dope, and then they found an unregistered gun in the glove box. I mean—they caught me. So I went to classes for a year. I paid cab fare, I paid for the classes, I paid attention. I went to anger management, and parenting, and drug classes. I did all that, and I still can't get a fucking job. What's the point?"

"You know—I never thought about it. But if they're going to make you pay your debt to society, so to speak, you would think that would rewrite your place. I mean why bother going through rehabilitation, why spend the money and the time if it doesn't mean anything? They may as well lock a guy up."

"I know. I'm no good on the outside world no more. Man—I fucked up a couple of times when I was young, and now I can't do anything about it. Now the only way I can make money is to sell. I keep trying to get a job. I worked at a restaurant. I worked at a club. I worked at Walmart. I worked at the college. But I can't get a break. They always find something after they hire me. I've never even fucked up on a job besides being late once in a while."

"Did you try calling the NAACP? I mean— isn't that exactly what they're there for? They are called *The Nation Associate for the Advancement of Colored People.*"

"Shit—I did that."

"And?"

"They said something about *they don't get into shit like that.*"

"Why the hell not? That sounds like it would be right up their alley. You're a black man who's right's have been twisted against what the system is supposed to stand for. You made mistakes, you took classes, and you got better. Man—you're the one that wants a real job. You want to work. And the system's forced you back into the dope trade when all you want to do is go straight."

"I know man. I'd quit in a second, but I got two kids and rent and bills to pay. Right now, it's the only thing I can do to put food on the table."

"Man—you've got basic civil liberty issue. What you're going through makes the system look bad. No offense, but I think the NAACP just wants to take on issues that they know they can win. They don't really want to fight for the state of rehabilitation, or help out black people. They have an agenda just like everyone else and they're not going to fuck with what's not in their interest."

"Yup."

"So what are you going to do?"

"I'm taking classes for my CDL license."

"How's that going?"

"Aright. It just ain't easy to study and raise a family and try to pay bills and everything in the meantime."

"Yeah—I guess so."

"Man. I don't know. I just want a chance somewhere. I mean—I don't really blame them for not wanting someone with child abuse and weapons charges working at a college around all those kids. But they should have looked at my damned application. Why'd I even fill it out if they weren't going to look at it?"

"Did they say anything about being hired pending a background check?

"They're saying they did. But man—that damned lady changes her story every day."

"Yeah? I don't know…"

"Man—It'll be alright once I get this CDL license."

"Think so?"

"Yeah. I hope so."

The streets are blank and undecipherable. Gas station. Forest. Gas station. We just drive in circles until we've hit every corner, and exercised every thought.

....

I hear James is doing better. His girl delivers pizza to us on a Monday night.

"Yeah—he's living downtown in those apartments by the library. He's hardly drinking anymore. Well—from James' perspective, he's hardly drinking. I think things might work out."

"Yeah thanks. Here, keep a dollar…"

Trying to imagine James sober is like trying to imagine a fish riding a bicycle. I see James' face pasted at the liquor stores. I see his name in lights at bars. I see convenience stores named in his honor. I see middle-eastern employees put through college from his midnight twelve-packing. I see waitresses going to ivy league schools on his bar tab. I see Tony Bennet making special appearances. I see congratulatory letters from Frank Sinatra's ghost, and Jim Beam's grand children.

I see brown glass on his forehead. I see dents in my ceiling. I hear roller coasters going down the stairs at night.

I remember pitchers of beers procured from local taverns ending up in our fridge in the morning, flat and separating. I see the stacks of grocery carts in the driveway, half eaten everythings, phones off the hook, and alarms ringing all day, all throughout town. I see him sleeping though judgment day, waking up hung over while everyone else is in their own little corner of heaven and hell. I see James lying in the rafters making stick figures in my ceiling.

She leaves in a flurry of pleasantries.

"Give me a call some time. I miss hanging out with you guys."

Tim recoils. Stephen grimaces. I nod politely and close the door.

....

Tim and I wander through a local park feeling frozen in time. I'm in the middle of some sea waiting for a true wind to show me true direction. Tim, meanwhile, is waiting for anything.

The air is starting to cool around us. Soon these old oak trees will be home to silver icicle fingers and white winter snow caps. Soon the swamps will be skating rinks, and the beaches will be undistinguishable from the rest of the forest.

We walk over a wooden bridge, and through an endless array of trails that occasional break into cornfields, modest housing developments, and soaring electrical towers. At a clearing, we climb trees to a private beach where Tim lights a hollowed out metal cigarette and takes two drags.

"It's nice out."

"It won't be for much longer. This is the end of it all, Charlie."

"Oh—I don't mind cold too much. I don't mind the snow. The snow comes, the college goes, our friends go, all those girls that we haven't talked to—that we even haven't met. They all go. We get snow. It's not exactly a fair exchange. But it's something. I take it there are no new leads this semester?"

"Even if there were, I don't think I'd have the energy to do anything. I'm just—frustrated. I want something to work."

Tim's teeth clench and his eyes roll back a little. His muscles, veins, and temples become tight. His left leg shakes like a wind up toy stuck against a wall. I can still see him crawling out of his own skin. I can still see him trying to escape.

I take a drag of the hollow cigarette. The lights, the leaves, the shine on the water—everything is softer. Gentler. Everything feels like it should have the texture of cotton, or fog. There aren't any edges in the forest. There are canopies and climbing oaks. There are marshes and frog groans.

Occasionally a jogger or a woman walking a dog passes us. Occasionally a fish jumps out of the water and hangs in the air.

Tim and I walk on.

At a dock closer to the outset, you can still see the sun setting, and there's nothing else in the world but the mergence of fire and water.

Crimson and gold currents grow rippling arms and dance. But everything else is still. Everything else is quiet. There is only the dancing light in blue, rippling fields.

I get into the car. We pass gas stations and yellow houses with white shutters. Tim turns on three wheels. He's singing along to the radio in a shaky, frail voice. I close my eyes and hum along.

What's next?

chapter eleven:

A Life in Letters.

To Charlie:

I got home a few nights ago. I had a great time in Canada, even though it rained the whole time. Everyone was wonderful. I was surrounded by so many different kinds of people. It really was amazing.

I guess I had a lot of time to think about everything. I thought about my job, about school, about the next year. About us. And I think we're coming from opposite sides. I think you want to carry me off in some romantic dream. And I'm flattered, really. But I don't feel like I have a voice in that dream.

I've lost so many friends before, because I wasn't willing to go that extra mile. And maybe you think I'm being cynical, or maybe you think I'm wrong. And maybe so many people shouldn't be telling me what I think anymore. Maybe I'm tired of all that.

You said you thought we were "uncomfortable" because of the crowds we carried ourselves in. But I like those groups. There's less pressure there. There's less of a spotlight over me. I can do that with my friends. Your friends want to make me into some celebrity or something and call me your "girl." It's nice that you've spoken so well of me. But it's also a little scary. And the other night at your house you said you felt like you "weren't there" or were distant, when I thought you were being just a little overbearing. I don't know how two people can have such a different take on the same situation. And I guess that every relationship is going to be a little uneven. But I definitely feel like I'm on the low end here.

I'm trying to do this without becoming a cliché. I guess I'm probably failing. But I'm trying to get everything out into the open now, because I feel like I haven't been doing that very well. Most of the time I haven't even known what or how to feel. And

I guess I acted pretty badly towards you sometimes because of that. But that's just my defense mechanism. If I can drive you away, I won't have to deal with all the confusion. It's a coward's way out, I know. But sometimes, I don't know what else to do.

You exist in your own world sometimes. You have your own set of rules. That scares me. I'm just starting to figure out who I am.

I got an email from Stephen today about your book. I saw your picture and I felt like crying. Sometimes I feel like you want too much from me. I don't think I can ever live up to what you've imagined me to be.

Being out in nature for two weeks made me want to be self-sufficient again. I guess I just can't do that in a relationship. Not right now. Not with you. I don't know if this all sounds like complete garbage to you, or if you think I'm being vindictive or spiteful or something. But I don't mean to. Really, I don't know what I mean to do anymore. I think I got lost again. With you. I don't know who that girl is that you've made me out to be. I know who the girl in the woods was. She was independent. She was functional.

I guess I just want to say that I think I should be single right now. I don't know what else to say. Maybe I'll talk to you later.

-Grace

To Grace:

Where earth is stolen or misplaced, there is always more earth. Where time feels threatened, there is always more time. It probably doesn't matter. And no, I'm not angry at you. That's not really my nature. But I understand, maybe better than anyone I know, what it's like to be confused, and what it's like to get hurt.

What I meant by distant was nature, conversation, and mentality rather than stature. I know I sat next to you awkwardly holding your hand—holding it like it was some life raft in the middle of an islandless ocean. Admittedly, that was rather overbearing—like a kid holding desperately to a parent's hand in a crowd, or like, "look everyone, she's really mine!" So, we're not so different in that view.

And the few people self righteous enough to call you "my girl" or else exclaim, "Oh! We've seen your picture!" are the same people the rest of us are usually telling to "shut the hell up." I said a few words about you because my friends asked about my romantic ties. I told them there's this girl who I over-identify with, and that there has been some small progress. But I also told them that there's been plenty of doubt and stalling. Basically, "there's this really great girl, I don't know..."
That's as far as I went.

And I don't know how or why I give off the impression that I want you all to myself. I'm sure I've offered my company in your times of hiding. I'm sure I've said things that might sound exclusionary. Truth is, before the summer started, I was holed up with one girl for an awful long time. Truth is, I value the hell out of my own independence. And surely, I can't say I wouldn't love to call you "my girl," but that doesn't mean the division of personal space must be eradicated. I want space. I need space. I have big things to do. I have ambitions that necessitate freedom. I need my own time to compose, conjure, create, and conceive. Like I said, I've been in this cabin in the woods with one woman and no oxygen and no friends.

Please don't think I'm asking for your time entire. I only want to add to you. I'm not here to subtract. I don't want to take you from friends, or projects, or ideas, or space, or travel. I had a great time these last three weeks. I thought you'd hang over my head. I thought I'd be more confused. Althea sent me a picture of you. I'm not sure how long ago it was taken. You were smiling on the couch. You had that smile that's almost too big to be real. Every now and then I'd look at it and smile back. And that's all I ever needed. And I got an amazing amount done.

And the book is doing well, and friends and fences have been mended, and everything is looking up—

And I don't feel awkward or confused anymore. You're a girl. You're a rather amazing one, but you're still just a girl. I spent my summer with other women whose face and skin and shine amazed everyone. But you're the only one with anything below the surface. When I met you, I suppose I retreated a little bit. I felt like it would be too cheap to simply smile and be easy in front of the first girl I've met in a long time that's actually deeper than the rain on the road. But I understand now, how human you, I, all of us are.

So if you want me, I'll be here, and around, and human. And I'd be thrilled to satisfy those easy levels, and allow for the space between us to feed those youthful desires for freedom. And I don't want your freedom. I only want a small piece of you heart. A picture. A last call. The rest belongs to you, and the world.

take care—

-charlie

To Charlie:

Thank you.

I'm sorry to make such a big deal of things. I'm just so used to running at any sign of a relationship. It's really the only way I know how to react anymore.

Anyway, thanks for trying to understand me.

I've been sooo busy lately. But I'm sure I'll talk to you soon.

-Grace

To Grace:

Thanking me for trying to understand you is like thanking a fish for having gills. I try to understand everybody. It's a side effect of a parentless childhood.

It just so happens that I beat a kitten to your lips over a tin roof and summer stars one faithful night—and that that, and the ensuing evening were the only honest romantic moments of the entire season. Maybe it's just my idiot-loyalty that rears its head and attaches itself to the art that occasionally appears behind a pretty face. But where other women held their diamonds overhead and their marble exteriors, you (for one still moment) held my heart. For that, it is even more automatic that I bear with the many moments of confusion you've caused subsequently.

Other than that, I don't expect anything save for sleep and death. They seem to occur rather naturally at the end of the day...

And hey—remember when our existence went outside of paper?

take care—

-charlie

....

Tim walks in the door at nine on a Friday.

"Hey man—is there anything going on tonight?"

"No one told you?"

"What?"

"There's a party at Grace's. It's her roommate's birthday or something. We're all going."

"Oh, great. Should I even bother?"

"Umm—yeah. Why not? Fuck`em!"

"Yeah. Why not?"

I call Ethan and tell him about the party. He sounds vaguely excited and promises to meet me there.

Tim, Sid, and I show up an hour later and begin drinking immediately. I ignore Grace as best as a wounded animal can his vice. I smile and I nod. I tell amusing stories to people I don't know.

Grace and the girls start playing drinking games in the kitchen. Their shouting and body language comes off as oddly exclusionary. The men, as a result, stand apart in stoic circles in the living room.

"What's the hell's going on here, Tim?"

"I don't know, but I'm not fucking going in there. They'll tear us apart!"

"Christ man—this is like some lame middle school dance where the guys and girls stand on opposite sides of the gym for four hours."

"I know. I think we're leaving pretty soon. This is eerie."

"I don't blame you."

Grace smiles wide within the sea of shouting women. I can make her out every now and then.

Tim and Sid make a run for it. Just then, Ethan bursts through the front door with a six-pack of beer and a suitcase full of records. Ethan is always the perfect antidote to bullshit. If nothing else—he'll manufacture his own that is far worse—far more absurd than anything else around him.

"Man, you came just in time."

"Man, d`you want a fucking beer?"

"Damn right I do. Man."

"Goddamn man this party is looking rather lame."

"Yeah—how `bout that box of records."

"I dunno—I don't think these people would understand any of this."

"That's exactly the point."

We commandeer the stereo and start flipping through cds. Ethan plays thirty seconds of Duke Ellington, a minute and a half of Fugazi, three of Captain Beefheart, and two of some random indie rock band. His patience is that of a kindergartener on Benzedrine. I keep drinking his beer and rolling around on the floor laughing at the voices in the other room that must be wondering what the hell we're doing to their poor stereo.

"Hey—this isn't *Destiny's Child*!"

"No shit!"

Eventually, we're thrown off the stereo. Ethan avenges himself by redoubling his drinking efforts. I, meanwhile, take a large lamp from the corner when no one's looking and replant it in the yard.

"What the hell didja do that for?"

"I don't know—man—I figured it's something you would've done."

"Are you trying to get me in trouble?"

The birthday girl walks into the living room with a large bottle of Yagermeister.

"Anyone dare me to drink this?"

"No!!!"

"Too bad!" She empties half the bottle down her throat and proceeds to fall over. By now all the girls have liberated themselves from the kitchen. Curiously, a number of them have managed to acquire water guns.

I wrestle one away from the inebriated birthday girl.

There's one other attractive girl in the whole dammed place. I shoot her in the neck.

Just then, the birthday girl recovers and tackles me from behind, knocking me into the stereo cabinet. Delia and Grace rush over, dismantle the stereo, and escort it quickly from the room.

I lay on the floor, bruised, but laughing.

A minute later, someone comes in through the front door and asks, "Why the hell is there a lamp on the front lawn?"

Ethan and I have a cigarette on the porch. The sky is always the same here, clear and sweeping from one end of the world to the other.

"This house is so different now."

"What do you mean?"

"Every other time I've been here it's been pretty quiet. There are always a few people and—there's always plenty of beer. But at the end of the night, it was always just Grace and I. Now, she doesn't even act like I'm here."

"Oh, boo-hoo buddy."

"What?"

"Quit your fucking complaining."

"Well how the fuck am I supposed to act?"

"I don't know. Just don't act like you're the only one who's ever had a fucking bad day. It's such bullshit."

"But—goddamnit—it's real."

"Yeah, I know it's fucking real. But it happens. Now fucking get over it and quit whining. You sound like an asshole."

"Are you serious?"

"Damn right, I'm serious."

"What—just like that, I'm supposed to cheer up and smile."

"Well, why the hell not."

"It's not that easy…"

"It is if you don't dwell on things all the time."

"Maybe for you…"

"Hey—I'm no different. I have bad days too, you know."

"Yeah, but they never hang on you like they do…"

"Well, why d`you let them?"

"I don't fucking know any other way. It's not that easy…"

"I don't know man. You just shouldn't let that shit get you down all the time. It happens to everybody."

"I'm going to get another beer."

"Yeah, you do that buddy…"

Inside, Delia and Althea are busy quoting *Saturday Night Live* skits with the girl I shot. She looks younger than everyone else there. She looks like the world hasn't run her over so much yet.

"Hey, Charlie, you know Audrey, don't you?"

"Audrey—no. Nice to meet you."

"You too…"

I grab another beer and sneak out the back. Grace, the birthday girl, and another are piled up in the backyard laughing. I tell the pile goodbye to their amusement, and drive away.

Sun Setting begins with a sad string section and a single French horn. When the strings fade, a stark acoustic guitar enters and a solemn voice sings:

Now I've fallen in deep,

Slow silent sleep
It's killing me,
I'm dying—

To Charlie:

I'm hiding out at Cordelia's house trying to think of something to say. I ran into James the other night, and he apologized rather vigorously for "putting his foot in his mouth" and for calling me your "girl" and everything. He seemed pretty upset about it, which makes me think you were pretty upset with him. It really wasn't that big of a deal, Charlie. I guess I overreacted a little bit, but I was also kind of flattered that you'd think of me that way. I was just a little surprised at the time. I didn't really know how to react. I guess I was just on edge about everything moving so quickly anyway, and that was kind of the boiling point.

I hope you don't think I was ignoring you the other night. I didn't mean to. Having all those people at my house was kind of strange for me, and I was just trying to have fun with my roommate on her birthday. I really don't know what to do about everything now. I know I need to talk to you at some point...

Anyway, I really don't know where I'm going with this, and now I'm being badgered to get the hell out of here. But I'll try and call you soon, I swear. I'm sorry for all the confusion I've caused.

And remember Charlie—you're a writer. There is no existence outside of paper.

-Grace

To Grace:

James, I may feel bad for the awkwardness, or our contributions to it. But only because it's an unnecessary side effect of two people who seem to care for and respect each other regardless of our poor movements toward romance. I'd like to state at the hour of honesty (5:43am) that any involvement you have in my life would be welcome and worthwhile. Don't think that I'm not terrified too of the future, or of my identity, or time, or bad influences. I'm pretty busy guarding my own mind from stillness and regression.

Anyway, it's good that you're flattered that I think highly of you to my friends who appear in bars.

And I wasn't really too offended that I didn't get to talk to you at the party. I know how meaningful your girls are to you. And I'm grateful that you have such good friends. You're lucky to have people like that.

And I had fun at the party observing the odd rituals of college women and Destiny's Child records, and in taking part in cabinet crashing and water fights, not to mention all the confused faces we created with Ethan's odd musical choices.

Anyway, the last thing you and I should be is distant or awkward. Press pause or stop or rewind at anytime. Press play at any time. I'm in no need now of marathon movies while the sun is still out and the air still so warm.

God—I wish my brain worked in obvious sentences— "You're a great girl. I enjoy spending time with you. We should do it again sometime. However, wherever."

Good? No pressure? Cup of coffee? Talk about books or middle western trade tendencies? Laugh at a bad movie or throw bread at ducks? I swear I don't always have to be a dry poet.

Anyway, I'll probably talk to you soon.

take care—

-charlie

· · · · · · · · · ·

Grace calls a few nights later.

"What's going on?"

"Not much. I have a little bit of work to do, but..."

"You're stalling?"

"Yeah."

"Well—do you want to cut out for a while?"

"Cut out?"

"What—is that too archaic a term?"

(Laughter)

"So, do you want to get out of the house?"

"What were you thinking?"

"Canoe ride."

"Canoe ride?"

"Canoe ride."

"At this hour?"

"Sure. This is the best time."

"Alright."

"Really?"

"Yeah!"

"Great! Do you want me to swing by?"

"Sure!"

"Alright. I'll be right there."

I change my shirt, wash up a bit, brush my teeth, and add shoes to the back seat of my car. And I catch myself smiling in the driveway.

Henry would call this "Vedantic karma" (Samsara). Radiohead would sing, "Everything in its right place". Maslow would call it the third hierarchy. Either way, I show up on her doorstep cleansed, shoeless, and in a great mood.

Grace opens the door and motions me in. Delia and her boyfriend are busy sitting on the floor playing Nintendo Jeopardy. I talk to them while grace readies her footwear. A minute later, she comes back in the room and claims a seat. We scream answers until Delia finally pulls in a victory.

And then her other roommate comes in and Grace stalls. And Delia and her boyfriend play another game. And we watch and laugh. And I ask Grace if she'd like to go. And she says yes, and leaves the room for a minute.

And she stalls. And they play another game and we watch and laugh. And another. And she stalls. And finally Delia, her boyfriend, and the former birthday girl are all looking at me with sad knowing faces as Grace puts on her pajamas and curls up on the floor.

I insert a cigarette between my naked lips and excuse myself into the night.

And I'd say I'm through, and *fuck her* if I didn't *care*, if I didn't *believe* I cared. All I ask is moment in a century, or five minutes without a fucking shield.

I don't understand. I don't understand anything anymore.

I pick up the phone and pull its umbilical cord free from the wall.

chapter twelve:

Perspective.

My head hurts. It pulses in that sort of dull morning-after throb. My neck is stiff and the rest of my body is utterly uninclined to motion. Last night I cleaned for four hours. I wiped a year of dust away from the bookshelves and stereo cabinets. I cleaned under couches and over sinks. I threw out the rotten fruit and swept the sugar, sorted spices, and tore down the old beer effigies in favor of Eve's black and white photographs.

Tim came home after midnight.

With Tim came the smoke. And with the smoke came the lemon-scented stereo and microwave pizzas. And after indulging, we all sat like basket cases around the television.

The shower turns on in the next room. Through the wall I can hear Tim singing random parts from old U2 songs in a cracking voice two octaves above his normal speech. I turn on comedy central and languidly fall back into bed.

A minute later the phone chirps intrusively. I groan and get up after six rings to answer to the frenzied voice of my father

"Charlie—are you watching TV?"

"Yeah…bad British improv…I think it's…"

"Charlie—turn on the news." I follow. Twin towers are on fire. "Charlie," he says in a low, solemn voice like Orson Welles in *War of the Worlds*, "we're under attack."

Immediately the hair on the back of my neck stands up, and shivers are hurled like missiles everywhere else.

The air in my already abused lungs stops. My head—throbbing—shakes awake.

"Fuck!" is all I can manage. "Fuck!" I gasp heavily, realizing that the room is becoming smaller. I throw open the door, disoriented, and stumble into the living room.

My father continues in the voice of Charles Foster Kane, "the world trade center is gone. Both buildings. Gone. The Pentagon is on fire. Watch for a while. Catch up. I'll call later."

Silence—

Tim shuffles, unaware in the bathroom. I start banging on the door

"What is it?"

"Tim! Jesus! Tim—get out here man. Fuck! We're under attack!" He throws open the door and runs into the living room. "The world trade center is gone man. The Pentagon...on fire..."

We are transfixed to the television.

Newscasters are biting back disbelief. Stories studied for months have been buried forever. For a minute, it's not like the news at all. For a while it's all pure human shock. You can see the uncertainty in the eyes of the broadcasters, set adrift without cue cards or script notes. All they have are pictures of America on fire.

But the images on the screen aren't real. They can't be. Two buildings tunnel easily into the ground like cement earthworms. They show this over and over again until the images of the bodies falling along with bricks and steel are burned into our brains.

This can't be real. Soon some action hero will appear and fly out the injured. And then he'll bomb the bad guy, and get the girl. And then the credits will give way to the houselights and the lanes of popcorn and juju and cola covered floors. And the double doors will open up into hills of red checkered carpet. And then we'll all be back in the real world, standing between the quarter cranes and the bathrooms. And we'll all walk through the food courts and discount clothing stores. We'll buy vibrating sofas, and cup holders. We'll walk by beaded teenagers and lipstick-laden business women in power suits carrying gourmet coffee in sad styrofoam containers. We'll watch as they march back to their safe corner cubicles, in a safe world that worries about tax refunds and charter schools. They'll stroll calmly into that world that argues for 401ks, retirement homes and eventual prescription drug programs. They'll crawl into old age easily and quietly against the southern seas and panhandles in island homes. They'll drink margaritas in canvas folding chairs, their cell phones tucked away in closets in four-star hotels. That's America. That's what we've come to believe is *real*.

This isn't real. This can't be.

Tim and I are shaking our heads. There is no other response. Our people are being used as bullets. Our security is shattered. There are no more oceans. There is no more need for missile defense. They'll crawl into our beds at night, and use the very genius knives that came with the new refrigerator bought on installment plans to cut the freedom from our hearts. They'll chain us to our ergonomic office chairs and throw us into our kidney-shaped swimming pools. They'll drown with the very ease to which we've become so accustomed.

Tim and I are shaking our heads. There is no other response. Our people are being used as bullets.

An hour ago I woke up, and all I wanted was a girl and cheeseburger.

Eve comes in twenty minutes later and joins our zombie world of revolving images. Every now and then one of us opens our mouths but nothing seems to come out. Nothing is worth saying. No words could match the images.

Our tongues hang on the newly cleaned carpet. Are lungs are filled with mortar. This doesn't happen in America. We have lean, mean, fat grilling machines. We have rotisserie ovens and microwaves. We have eight thousand channels, all night convenience stores, and live music seven nights a week.

And I haven't even worked a job in months! I don't live in reality! It's not fair to make me live in reality.

"I think I'm going to get drunk."

"Charlie—don't. We might have to evacuate. There might be more."

"WELL I CAN'T TAKE THIS STRAIGHT. I NEED ICE, A FUCKING LIME, A TWIST OF FOG."

"They just said 50,000 people work and visit there daily."

"This is the worst thing that's ever happened. This is it. These were innocent people."

"They were capitalists."

"They were secretaries and mail clerks! They were parents and grandparents! Their kids were in day care! What the fuck?"

"Don't get drunk Charlie. Wait a little while."

Stephen walks in.

"Are you guys watching this?"

"It's on every channel."

"Is this shit real?"

"I don't know yet."

"Fuck that—I'm rolling a joint. Who's with me?"

Tim and I are.

"This is the most peaceful fucking thing we can do. We're going to get stoned and sit around a table——shit every channel?"

"Every channel."

Stephen's fingers shake against the paper. We watch him with a great deal of reverence, as if he were the first man in space.

Afterward, we all walk to the grocery store across the street. It's hollow inside, but at least there are no televisions.

What can my stomach hold? The dope helps a little.

Tim gets a sandwich, a bag of pretzels, a carton of soda, microwave lasagna, and a pack of cigarettes.

My father never calls back. There's nothing more to say.

....

The news is on wall to wall for days. The toll of *dead and missing* is updated with more frequency than a stock ticker.

Soon Bono is weighing in. By Wednesday, Sting is on VH1 bihourly. By Friday all the cars outside carry American flags.

A local pizza shop run by two Arabic brothers is questioned. Their ad in the yellow pages shows a picture of the world trade center behind a pair of spinning pizzas.

Fox News says England is pissed. Mexico, Canada, Israel, Germany, and Italy are also pissed. Even France is pissed.

We're all hearing names we'll never learn to pronounce. It's like Spanish class without the annoying cartoons and workbooks. Maybe we'll have taco day on Friday.

Tim comes and goes and nods his head and sighs. Stephen hasn't gotten past pure rage since that joint.

It's strange. I've felt like this before. My heart's been broken. My security has been shattered. But it was never this *real* before. It was never this big. It was never televised before. It was never run over by an expert panel. It never merited tribute concerts and presidential speeches.

My entire generation has grown accustomed to experiencing horror safely within the confines of our own heads. We always had pills for our troubles. We always sat on comfortable couches and listened to soft voices reassure us that the occasional feelings of uneasiness are normal.

My father remembers his town on fire during the civil rights struggle in the sixties—but those were courthouses—and the fires were for equality. What, then, were those planes for?

A guest on a talk show says, "one man's freedom fighter is another man's terrorist." I fish the phone out of the couch and throw it through the television.

....

I dream I'm in an office in a high rise building, staring at a familiar picture of a girl.

She's doing it again. She's drifting off. She's remembering her mother's face, and the way it looked almost lifelike in the garage that day, slumped over in the driver's seat. I can see it in her eyes each time we pull in the driveway to visit her father, or each time she sees the bare white walls that were once smiling photographs in neat wooden frames.

Her picture sits awkwardly on the desk. She took that picture. She let nothing come between herself and the camera. Maybe that's why the eyes still look real even now, two-dimensional and behind glass.

A long manila envelope is deposited onto the desk. It's funny that mail actually comes from somewhere. When you're at home, the mail is a mystery. It appears in a little box by the door the way quarters used to appear under your pillow after mother played the tooth fairy. Here the tooth fairy's name is Jim. Jim has gout and a penchant for banana bread.

I really don't know how I ended up here. I remember going to these wild bonfires full of painters and playwrights and shop teachers. I remember the wood that came each time in the same red pickup, and that one time my girlfriend's contacts were warped by the heat from the fire.

I'd go home after all this and type what I saw, wake up a little after noon and dig into a James Joyce novel. I'd spend the quieter evenings chasing female photographers, or sitting on the front porch contemplating streetlights.

The boss walks by and I pretend to type something about "a new kind of car company." To my left is a propped-up picture of a red sedan with cruise control and leather seats that smell like mother did after she married into money. The picture is frowning at me now.

Hammond Emery lingers near the water cooler, waiting for the clock to turn ten hours over. He should be here. He was practically raised in a cubicle. His father was an old ad man himself. When he got out of school with that phony communications degree, he followed the old man here for lack of anything better to do. Now it's twenty years and he's still staring at the clock.

Now the picture is looking at me the way she used to. Her head is cocked slightly to the right, and I can almost make out that little glimmer that shone before the medication stole her last light, before it took 500 milligrams to fall asleep. She was barely eighteen before her life was extinguished by her own goddamned mother.

I shouldn't be here. I should get us both out of office land. Maybe we could start fresh somewhere away from the city, maybe somewhere where long lazy driveways negate garages. Maybe we could move somewhere slower where your mind can wander, or where the skies lack just enough city light to see the stars. I wonder when was the last time she saw stars.

Now the picture is frowning again. I strike three keys and the computer shuts down. I stand up as if stretching, and tuck the photograph into a flimsy brown briefcase. She's only three blocks away. I might even catch her in the street, or in the lobby just on her way in. I'll catch her just outside and convince her to call out. Maybe go see that movie she won't shut up about. Maybe tomorrow I'll call about that new job.

Somehow I can't help but think the picture is finally grinning.

The clock says 8:49. But Hammond isn't looking at the clock anymore. Rather, he's searching for the source of that rumbling.

The water cooler is dancing. It leaps up like an excited ocean, and everyone around us is looking past Hammond and towards the invisible rumbling.

Now the hair on the back my neck stands straight up. And then the rumbling emerges to our left. Its furious nose points straight for the indignant clock that has stopped forever.

And the picture in my briefcase groans as I close my eyes.

chapter thirteen:

Ethan and Oxycodone.

Ethan lives alone on the outskirts of town in an ancient two story house. Just inside the long wooden door is a large, headless painting of a nude woman done with such detail that you could almost—

To the left is a poster of Bo Jackson.

To the right is an old green metal desk equipped with a thrift store typewriter.

There's a gigantic black heater in the center of the room. There are chairs, paintings of stuffed animals, tape recorders, ash trays, magazine clippings of grave-faced old women, monster gloves, guitar amplifiers, keyboards, books, magazines, couches, tables, normal things, bizarre things, ironic things, nonsensical things and ridiculous things. But everything seems to have its place here, even if it's just to be absurd. It's as if every inch of pop culture has been gathered together two by two and forced to live and get along in this old, dusty house. You can't decide whether to laugh or furl an eyebrow.

Ethan doesn't furl anything. This is his planet.

Upstairs, we listen to old records and get drunk. Ethan spins heavy metal with disco, indie rock with Burt Bacharach, and rap with show tunes.

I sit on a chair in the corner with a beer.

"Rawk and roll, brother. You got a smoke?"

"Yeah, here. You know, I think you're the only person in town who even has a fucking record needle?"

"Come on, man. It can't be that bad."

"I think it is. I'm starting to."

"Then why don't you fucking leave?"

"You make it sound so easy."

"Why not? What's holding you here?"

"That's a good question."

"No—really."

"I don't know. One month it's a girl. The next month, I'm broke…"

"Whatever. I've never seen you work a day, and you've always got cash."

"Yeah, well I found out that money really does grow on trees."

"It's the government, man. They hide everything."

"The truth is out there."

"The truth is in George Bush's underwear drawer."

"I wonder what else he keeps in there."

"I don't know. Coke, supreme court justices, midgets…"

"Midgets?"

"Yeah man, every president has midgets."

"Damn executive privileges."

"Damn right!"

"What the hell were we talking about?"

"You being a whiny little bitch."

"And midgets."

"Well, yeah…"

Ethan pulls out a pipe and lights up. The smoke curls up into the dim lamplight. For a minute, I think I can see it dancing.

"What are we listening to?" Ethan throws a record jacket in my lap. "This isn't bad."

"Of course not."

"You hungry?"

"A little."

"Let's go over to the college."

"And do what?"

"I don't know. Break into the piano lab, pick up undergrads, steal toilet paper, I'm restless."

"Alright. You driving?"

"I think I can see straight. Say—isn't that Richard Nixon?"

"Fucking republican."

"Fucking journalist. You know, if left out in the wild, we'd be natural enemies. I'd probably have to hunt and kill you."

"That's 'cause you're a gun-toting slave of the NRA lobby. Man."

"Oh, yeah."

The road ahead is empty. The campus is empty. All the lights are out. Everything is brick and starlight, sun-bleached picnic tables and overstuffed bulletin boards.

In Fulton Hall, Ethan bangs out a series of seemingly unrelated chords on a shimmering black piano. I butcher a *Rolling Stones* song in the adjoining room.

The walls are padded like nut houses in the movies. Each room has a coat rack and an extra chair. But nobody ever comes in here. This is the last, great, untouched place in town.

Ethan winks and hands me a couple of pills.

"What are these?"

"Oxycodone. Pain killers."

I take two.

Brick and Starlight. We stumble around like two things that just crawled out of the sea. Anyone who saw us wouldn't have mistaken us for human beings. We have tentacles and dorsal fins. Our tongues hang out through our eyes at the statues that look like people.

"Hey! Buddy—you got a smoke? Good lord, he's naked?"

"That's a statue, man."

"Good lord, they're everywhere."

"It isn't safe here this time of night. We'd better head to higher ground."

"Good idea. But we'd better stop talking. They might try and follow us. Maybe we could work out a series of blinks."

"Jesus Christ, man. Get a hold of…"

"Diner!"

"What?"

"That new diner. It's right ahead."

"Rawk and roll, brother."

Inside the diner is a table of ten, maybe fifteen police officers having eggs and coffee. We're seated in the corner next to them.

"Ethan—your tentacles…"

"Did I say Jesus Christ?"

"Not since we walked into hell."

"Jesus Christ."

"I think he's laughing at us."

"He's doing something."

The cops know what we're up to. They can smell it. Ethan's eyes are bright red slits, and I keep muttering and stumbling back and forth from the bathroom, getting lost in the process. Ethan just sits there with his head down drinking coffee.

Eventually we order food—hot, greasy, awful, wonderful life-giving food. The eggs melt right off my fork. The bacon hangs in the back of my throat, and the orange juice flows throughout my body like cool blood cells. I feel flushed, full, heavy, warm, and powerful. Meanwhile the police have surrounded us in a small diner at three in the morning. They caught us out in public looking and smelling like escaped French madmen. But I don't give a damn anymore. My skin just crawled off and stumbled toward the bathroom, but I don't care. The table and the walls are rocking back and forth like a buoy. But I don't care.

If I ate this in any other state, my body would reject it immediately. My arteries would clog and my heart would become something resembling petrified wood. But this food is saving our lives now. I'm convinced of it.

"This is pretty damned good."

"This is art."

"I'd pay to see a fry cook next to Picasso."

"Fuck Picasso. Next to hash browns, he's a hack."

The police leave two by two. Each one glares at us on the way out.

The last pair seems to be lingering by the doorway. The walk in for a toothpick, or the toilet, stare us down determinedly and then walk back out. They're waiting for us. They want us to pay the check and drive away. They want to catch us with dead bodies and eight hundred pounds of heroin in the trunk. Luckily my car's back on campus, a half mile or so away.

"Fuck Picasso," Ethan mutters. The last cop walks away.

Back at the house, I crawl into a large closet in the hallway. Ethan throws me a blanket and a few pillows, and turns on the BBC morning news on a small radio in the bathroom.

chapter fourteen:

E v e r y b o d y   h a s   b e e n   B u r n e d .

Will Self walks into the living room a little awkwardly. His hat is bent backwards, his shoulders are slouched, and his stomach projects heavily past the rest of his body even though he's slumped forward quite a bit.

Isaac, Sid, and I are busy with a case of beer. Will sits down and listens to the end of Isaac's story.

"…so I bent her over the kitchen counter and starting railing the shit out of her right there." Isaac swings his right arm in large circular slapping gestures. The room erupts.

"You know I've had my share of pretty hot women guys…"

The room stops dead.

"Will—what the fuck are you talking about?"

"I'm serious man. Before I moved down here, I used to tear some shit up. I had a lot of nice girls…"

"And how many of these women were relatives of yours?"

"Man it's not like that."

"You know the voices in your head don't count right?"

"God—shut up Isaac! Why does it always have to be like that?"

"Why are you always so full of shit?"

I have to jump in. "It's just—since you've been here man, we've seen you with one girl. And she really wasn't much to write home about…"

"Yeah, well back home I used to tear some shit up. Man—Fell—I used to get girls that would put any of yours to shame."

"Oh come off it Will, we've all seen that fucker in action. He does alright for himself."

"There you go. Stroke my ego…"

"I'm just saying…"

"Look guys— I'll bet I slept with—like twenty two girls."

The room erupts in laughter.

"Hey, move the decimal over…"

"Two places to the left."

"Man, I can name them. Jennifer, Lisa, Kim, Michelle, Angela, Maria…"

"Uvula, Chlamydia…"

"Shut up!"

"Rosy Areola…"

"Freeda Beast…"

"Shut up! You can all go to hell!"

Will knocks over his chair and storms out of the house. Isaac and I are on our sides laughing.

"Can you believe that piece of shit?"

"Yeah—I know. I'd better go check on him though…"

Will is sitting in his truck, sulking. The engine's on, but he's not moving.

"What d`you want? Man—I though you guys were my friends…"

"We are, man. You just leave yourself open all the time. You have to realize that we wouldn't respect you any more if there were four or four hundred women. Don't disturb your senses for our faith in numbers. It doesn't matter."

"I know. It's just that it's not easy being here. I'm not used to this. I hate this fucking town."

"Will, this town is every town. This is every small town in America. It's just not easy anywhere."

"I know. But at least in the city you can disappear…"

··········

Stephen sits in the center of his room surrounded by cardboard boxes.

"You're really going to do this, aren't you?"

"I love her, Charlie. I have to."

"Man, you just met her *four* weeks ago."

"Oh, I know. I never said this wasn't a stupid move. Heheh. But hey—I haven't done anything stupid in a few weeks. It's about that time."

"It is New York."

"Yeah. I always wanted to live in the city…"

··········

Ethan arrives with his usual armful of beer. We examine a copy of Carl Sandburg's *Honey and Salt* that I just liberated from a local bookstore.

"forget everything you ever heard about love
for it's a summer tan and a winter windburn
and it comes as weather comes to you and you can't change it"

Later we listen to records and stare at the ceiling, drunk. Steven is leaving us. I can hear him packing in the next room. He comes and goes like the weather, or like love.

Will is the opposite. He walks against the weather and ends up stranded here. Ethan doesn't really ride the weather, or go against it. Ethan is the weather. He is predictably unpredictable.

I, for now, am abandoning the weather. I still have sunburns and windburns. But I'm due to stare at the ceiling for a while.

....

In the morning Stephen is gone. I sweep the dust he's left and move into his room.

In a few days, Able will take his place. For now, Tim and I enjoy the static and the silence.

In a bottle, it's easy to forget that the sky is falling. I wanted to be a saint this week, but I keep medicating myself.

Rome, and her magic are in decline. Friends are frequent victims of misfortune. Mother has started taking pills. Grandfather is getting older and more lonesome.

Tim is getting at once more social, and more lonesome.

Henry has been dismissed from his steady.

James falls more often than the moon.

Even Dean calls. His voice, suspended forever on the answering machine, is cracked and quiet.

"Charlie...this is...Dean... I don't know..."

Grace is still gone.

It's raining in the wide world outside. And the mood is the weather is the mood. We are children without space to play, sun to shine, or mothers to comfort our defeated dreams.

I wanted to be a saint this week. I've had my cause for comfort. I beat the revolving inevitability. For a while.

For a while, I existed authentically. For a while I held beauty in my arms. I saw that decade smile.

It's raining outside. And the mood is the weather is the mood.

Epicureanism Reprise.

I don't know what it is about house sitting. Maybe television is responsible for those images of bikini-clad girls glued to our minds like so much stale beer on kitchen linoleum. Maybe too many movies embedded too many dreams of high school beer bashes in our heads. Maybe this is simply a pathetic attempt to hold on to the last threads of our adolescence. Either way, Tim's parents have left town, and a party is absolutely inevitable.

Ethan arrives at my house near midday with his saxophone player Crenshaw, his drummer Nigel, a large black bag filled with wigs, and an instant camera. I don't ask questions.

We visit our local liquor store and make the long drive to the outskirts of town.

At the house, I make friends with a bottle of vodka. Will, Tim, Sid, Jude, James, and Henry pass a joint in the kitchen.

Ethan raises a puzzled eyebrow. "Where are all the women, man?"

The room bursts into immediate laughter.

"I don't think these guys know any…"

"Charlie, call some freakin` women, for chrissakes."

I shrug my shoulders.

"Man. D`you guys at least have guitars?"

They do.

Ethan, Crenshaw, Nigel, and I man the instruments. Between Crenshaw's jug of wine and my bottle of vodka, we manage to play with all the grace of confused children. We only stop after Tim's yelled at us a fifth time.

The sun's going down slowly outside. The four of us raid the tool shed for a rake and a tennis ball. Once we've lost the tennis ball we use my car keys. They fly over the roof and into the neighbor's flowerbed.

Inside we watch the Game Show Network and convince Tim's little dog to chew on a large wooden duck.

The wine's almost gone, and Tim has kicked us off the guitars again. Crenshaw starts distributing wigs and dancing with the dog. You heard me right.

He takes pictures of himself with a polyester afro. The room is starting to spin.

Lorelei walks in.

Crenshaw drops his drawers and takes a picture to our mutual disgust.

Ethan starts a sermon. I don't pay attention to his words so much as I do his gestures. His eyebrows become very serious. His forehead wrinkles thoughtfully, and his head leans a little to the right.

Lorelei seems very impressed by all this.

Nigel is propped up in the hallway. He smirks crookedly with his eyes closed.

Crenshaw drops his pants and takes a picture to our mutual disgust.

Across the hall, strangers stumble into a dark bathroom.

"The light switch is a dial…"

"No—on the other wall…"

"Never mind."

I take a picture of Crenshaw and the dog sharing saliva. Ethan and I are on the floor.

Lorelei mistakenly drops the picture in front of Tim who is becoming dangerously drunk. He jumps up immediately.

"Motherfucker—stop molesting my dog!"
We all laugh thinking it all a joke. Crenshaw drops his pants to our mutual disgust.

Tim becomes serious. His fists are poised for a showdown. "Motherfucker! That motherfucker! He has no idea!"

He casts a heavy right hand into the wall. Tim has become serious. Everyone around him is whispering on his behalf. The veins in his forehead look like little earthquakes. He stomps his feet like a frustrated child.

I look to Ethan.

"We'd better get the hell out of here while there's still room to run." He nods. Lorelei bats her eyelashes. "Hey—d`you wanna come?"

"Sure. Let me get my bag…"

Ethan shoulders Nigel to the car. Lorelei pulls up behind us. Crenshaw shakes his head.

"Ain't none of ya` seen a grown man kiss a dog before? Fuck!"

The back roads are a blur. The car smells like wine and polyester wigs. We're drunk but out of booze, stoned but out of smoke. But halfway we realize that

we've taken the only pretty girl—okay, the only girl—
from a dull party.

We roar into the driveway. Ethan and the
others stumble clumsily towards the front door. Lorelei
leans out of her car.
"Charlie?"
"Yeah?"
"Do you want to go to my place?"
"Is that a question?"
"Should it be?"
"I don't know. It's not very hard to answer…"
"Charlie, are you coming or what?"
"Sure—sure. Hold on…"

I stumble over to the others.
"Uh—change of plans guys. She uh—she
invited me back to her place, and…"
"Yeah!"
"Get her man!"
"Wooooooooooooo…"
"Hey—whatrwe gonna do?"

Lorelei's house is quiet. I trip up the stairs. She
doesn't notice.
A minute later she's standing in the bedroom
doorway in a pair of boxers and a white t-shirt. Her
amber limbs leak out like suggestive smoke. I trip onto
the bed.

··········

I get home at seven in the morning. My head is
pounding. Three red lights blink unsympathetically in
the corner.

One: *"Two twenty two in the a.m. Crenshaw, I hope you're fucking there, cuz if I ever see you again, your head's gonna be fuckin taken off. Cuz I know what the fuck you said, and you're gonna fuckin die you punk-ass bitch…"*

Two: *"Hey Crenshaw! Dude, if you're there—you have no fucking idea. Bitch."*

Three: *"Hey Crenshaw. You're not gonna live too much longer…"*

I take a breath. Old Tim. Gentle, confused creature. Old friend. You've gone from the desperation that scratched till it bled, to these foolish threats aimed at an empty house. No one was even here. No one was here to hear your voice.
Is that what's really wrong? Do we have to hear your screams to understand? Gentle old friend. You make me aware of the mistakes we all make on bellies full of beer.

Two days later he walks in the door, dead sober.
"I'm sorry about the other night Charlie. I guess—I must have gotten out of hand. I know I did. But that fucker was taking advantage…"
"No. I don't want to hear any more about it. I don't want to relive any of it. No more, man." His head drops down like a disappointing child. "We make mistakes. One week you became violent to yourself. The next week you became violent to others. Crenshaw may've been acting off—but he didn't do anything to incite violence. Just—be careful—realize…"
"I know—I just…"
"No reasons. Just—no more, alright?"
"I know. No more drinking like that. I guess it's catching up on me."

What else can we expect when youth is tempered with fire? No more.

We smoke a cigarette on the porch to forget.

....

I live on porches smoking cigarettes for the five minutes of calm and reflection they provide. I'm best just after it starts to rain, and the sky isn't yet covered, and there's a hint of stars.

Drops of rain accumulate on the roof and make waterfalls. I wonder how many drops of rain my roof can hold. I wonder how the rain falls and never asks why.

Sometimes I want to be paved over with earth, ended. Sometimes I crave only silence—complete and terminal. Sometimes to be loved or to be important is far too grave or daunting to ever be worthwhile. Sometimes stacked instants of time become the weight heavy enough to burry a man even before he is gone. And yet I am still so young. How will I ever feel with fifty more years of time on my shoulders? How will I ever survive the generations forward?

I pick up the phone and call Cassandra.

"Charlie! I wasn't sure if I'd ever hear from you again."

"Yeah. I guess I've been a little busy here."

"Oh, I'm sure. What's up?"

"Well—have you eaten anything?"

"Not recently."

"Would you like to?"

"That—might be good."

"Good. Why don't you stop by, say in an hour?"

"Sounds great, I'll see you then."

Not the queen, or space aliens. Not Grace.

I peer through the blinds at the rain-soaked road. And suddenly I have the deep and unmistakable urge to run.

Instead, I juggle kitchen utensils and vacuum the living room. And I put the same Miles Davis record on the stereo, and I make the same salads. And I feel like I'm cheating on myself.

I light the same candles.

Cassandra arrives right on time. And she is lovely. And that does help.

"Wow. You did this in an hour?"

"Well, I keep everything in the closet. The whole thing actually folds up. Do you want to see?"

"That's alright. Can I sit down? Wow—this is actually really good."

After dinner we watch a movie designed to get girls like Cassandra into bed. I mechanically hand her another beer. She moves in a little closer. Her head sinks down to a pillow. I follow her altitude.

I wait like a rattlesnake in the brush. I produce just enough noise to make my presence known.

She doesn't run. Her straight blonde shimmering hair flows neatly down to the top of her shoulders. She smells like bottled springtime. She doesn't run. So I strike her in the neck.

She is a little surprised. But she leans in anyway.

....

She is young, tender, willing, watery, soft, vulgar, stone, sand, currents, shadows, calm, electric, breakfast, lunch, dinner, and desert. Her body flickers and dances like a candle, even though her wit freezes and holds it's cold shape.

When we round each other, she holds me in the air with her legs, fingers, eyelashes, lips, center—

We're like matches to oxygen, or swimmers between breaths. We are the last summer sweat, and the first autumnal falling.

....

A week later, she moves away to college.

On the second weekend, she drives back. I wait like a rattlesnake in the brush. She barely makes it into the house before I have her pinned to a wall. I know where to go now. I know her body well enough.

She moans and helps me shed cotton.

....

I go back to college as well. I sit in the same classrooms staring at the same lime-green concrete walls. The same teachers arrive late with questionable mugs.

The only difference is Eve walking beside me for two days a week. She carries four paintings at a time, knocking the unframed corners against doorways, and occasionally, dragging their bases against the floor.

She sporadically sends me reports of Lola.

"I saw her the other day, going into Two Dimensional Design..."

"Did she say anything?"

"No. She just frowned and ducked."

One day we run into Grace on the way to admissions. Her house is full of people and her classes are full of films. Eve nudges me towards her a little.

Grace walks with us up marble steps and down sandstone hallways. She spots Althea in line and tactfully manages to hide under her skirt. Eve and I spot Sid ahead of them and excuse ourselves.

··········

It's a nice, clear blue day. I'm walking toward the English department. An attractive girl in front of me is struggling with the door. She looks familiar. She holds the door for me.

Eve is inside at the other end. I hand her a drink spiked with whiskey. The girl from the doorway appears again. "Damn you walk fast." I do know her. She sits down next to Eve.

We watch the first fifteen minutes of *Hamlet* before leaving to play pool at a local bar.

On the way there we stop at Eve's house. Her mother is worried about her husband's lateness home. She makes a few calls as we eat tacos.

At the pool hall I see another girl I used to know. She is tall, slender, beautiful and empty. We talk to her briefly, and she pays a little attention to me, but not enough to get excited about.

We set up at a table opposite a pair of pill-boxed-hatted old black men who start giving us candid advice on everything from backspin to drink orders. They have an odd, grandfatherly sort of manner of speaking. And one of them—a rumpled old fellow who happens to be missing an arm, takes an instant liking to Eve.

I win the first two games and hand out cigarettes like they were hospital cigars.

A half hour later a group of girls walk in and claim a table about fifty feet away. One of them looks exactly like Lola. Her face, hair, and body are the same. She poses and frowns the same. She's even wearing the same red t-shirt Lola always wore.

Eve meanwhile calls her mother on a payphone by the bathroom. Everything is fine.

She comes back and wins a few games when I scratch on the eight, and one when I hit a couple in for her. I win the last game, and we say goodbye to our newly adopted grandparents and head off for parts unknown.

Later we stop by Lamont's house. He's playing videogames and ignoring us for the large part. His house is quiet, full of pictures of his kids. We drink whiskey and smoke a cigarette while talking about his temp job at Walmart, CDL license by the end of October, and Eve's new boyfriend's heavy metal band being crummy.

I call Ethan, and Eve and I buy beer and head to his house. He's playing the usual strange surreal deconstructed noise rock and rambling on about something in his own unique banter that twists like an artful snake, but never really seems to go anywhere. We start writing a poem on the old typewriter. Ethan and I are drinking boilermakers and getting high. I play his upright bass in the corner between verses.

Eve goes home. We go upstairs, listen to records and get high. At 3am, we wander out for cigarettes. Ethan wants to walk, but I can't make it three blocks in this condition. So I offer to drive.

At the store, Ethan buys a box of Ellio's pizza, a box of donuts, and a pack of unfiltered cigarettes. I buy a bag of popcorn.

Outside, an older black man on a bike starts talking to us about getting high. He asks where the party is. We give him bad directions.

Then a young black girl, maybe eighteen, approaches Ethan and asks if we can give her a ride. It's on the way, so we gladly oblige.

She tells her three male friends to jump in, and the four of them pile into the back. The girl stretches out across the guys.

One of them offers us drugs. We tell him we have enough, and that we don't "mess with powder". Ethan puts on the local hip-hop station. The kids in back sing along, laughing and dancing despite the cramped seating.

We let them out at a gloomy bend about mile or so from the store. Ethan gets out to say goodbye. I'm about to do the same when one of them grabs me from behind and shouts, "give me your fucking money!"

I gasp, "but—we were trying to help you…" He only tightens his grip around my neck. I can't breath. I can't breath to tell him he can have the goddamned money.

Everything's so foggy. Can I shake him? My hands won't let go of his around my neck.
He starts jabbing at the side of my head.

I slip out for a second and yell, "take the fucking money, here!" throwing $35 into the back seat. He grabs it and runs out.

Outside, Ethan's being beaten and choked by the other two. I hit the gas and run right for them. They scatter quickly, and Ethan manages to jump into the back seat.

We sit at his house for a few minutes in a shocked stupor, pacing about the living room. Ethan's wallet and keys are missing.

For some stupid fucking reason we get back in the car drive around, circling the block for the right street and bend. I spot Ethan's wallet in a ditch on Germania Circle, hop out and get it.

"Hold the car."

"You got it! That's it!"

Everything's there except for a few dollars and his credit card.

Ethan's neck is bruised badly. Back at the house he calls his credit card company to cancel, but only manages to get machines on the line.

Then we hide the dope, and call the police. I turn my car around to hide the expired tags. The officer arrives and takes our statement.

"They jacked up two other people tonight just like they did you. Same description and everything. Probably in it for the crack."

Ethan is unusually quiet for the rest of the night. He's baffled.

"Fucking niggers."

"Ethan?"

"They were. They were ignorant assholes. I don't care what color they were. Fuck them."

"Yeah, but…"

I know he didn't mean to use *that* word. Ethan would never say that. I refuse to believe he used *that* word.

We were being nice. We were being nice in a small town to a couple of tired looking, seemingly harmless kids that beat the fuck out of us, strangled us, and took our money. We were mugged in *anytown*. We were stupid and naïve, and we were proud that we had been able to exist that way. But those fuckers shattered Ethan's naiveté. They lost a great human being that day. They lost one of the last innocent, nice, harmless, reasonable people on the planet. And they did it for $35 and a credit card that won't ever work.

I fall asleep in Ethan's closet, covered in blankets and listening to early morning BBC radio.

....

A few days later, I'm back to stuffing envelopes full of query letters. I'm starting to become convinced that the postal service is in direct cohorts with the publishing industry. They come up with catchy phrases like, *attempted, unknown* and *moved, not forwardable* even though forwardable isn't even a word. They should be ashamed of themselves.

Cassandra calls me from her car phone, to tell me she's just seen the *Spin Doctors*.

"Aren't they dead?"

"No!"

"Why the fuck not?"

She's driving 100mph down the highway. She sounds like something from a Bukowski poem, "I *like* people and I *like* parties and I *like* to dance! And so do all my sisters, they'd drive 2000 miles to go to a party!"

My neck fucking hurts. I have a black eye now. It's two days later.

I call Ethan.

"We got pretty beat up, didn't we?"

....

The sky is clear tonight. Everything else is confused.

Stars come on good report cards and appear regularly on late night talk shows. Clouds come in cereal boxes. So do pieces of the moon.

Ethan and I still haven't recovered from the other night. He's taking pain killers for the injuries on his face and throat. He calls me from work every day to exchange bruises and confusion

Today I drove around town to see it for what it truly is—small. We have fourteen boat ramps, sixteen hotels, twenty shopping centers, and over sixty restaurants. I've been to every one of them. I've been to every bar. I've driven down every street.

But more than that—I feel like I've done everything. All my memories cast a shadow on this town that is becoming increasingly hard to shake. The shadow comes from a job and extends across an entire shopping center. This shadow comes from a girl and has brothers in several movie theatres, restaurants, and out of the way parking lots. That shadow dated my mother when I was eight. This one died when she was only fourteen.

Sometimes I drive past an old girlfriend's house just to see how little everything has changed. Most of them have long since moved away, and yet hardly a blade of grass has shifted in years.

Sometimes I drive by one of the houses we used to live in. That one still has chipped green paint. This one lost a tree. That one gained a shrub.

This one still has the same ditch at the end of the street that used to fill up so high with rain that we'd put on our bathing suits and swim. That one is still across the street from the dusty old ball field with a broken backdrop and hard sun scorched sand. Past the swing set, there's still a giant smiling ladybug bobbing

back and forth drunkenly on a rusty spring. Behind
that is the forest where we used to catch garter snakes
and scare the smaller kids with our ghost stories about
the old axe murderer who buried their misbehaving
sons under the bent oak tree that grew arms at dusk and
red eyes in the rain.

Sometimes I drive by Eve's house to see if the
light's still on in her bedroom. If it is, she's up painting
and listening to Joni Mitchell, or the Sundays.

Today I drove by the gas station where we
picked up those kids the other night. A couple of black
teenagers were sitting on the sidewalk scowling under
their ski caps and doo-rags. I wanted to do something
to them. I didn't know what—but my fucking throat
hurt, and those kids were just sitting there.

I saw a thirty year old black man walking down
the street. He glared at me as I drove by. Didn't he
notice the bruise under my left eye?

"Fuck your repressed class bullshit you fucking
band of hypocrites!"

I go to Lamont's house to get some perspective.
"Who is it?"
"Who the hell do you think it is?"
"What up Charlie? Come on up."
He's fighting with his girlfriend again while his
six month old daughter lay in a large pink play pen
staring up at a sea of singing stars.

"Man—it ain't like that! You know I just went
out to the damn club with my boys. I *can* still do that,
can't I? You ain't gotta be on my back every damn
second of every day…"

"I ain't trying to be on your back—but you've
got to find a fucking job."

"Don't I pay the bills?"

"Yeah, but…"

"Don't I? Alright then. What the fuck are you trying to worry about?"

She throws her arms up and walks into the bathroom.

"Damn. Sorry about that man."

"It's alright…"

"What 'cho doing?"

"Nothing really. I've just been driving around."

"You know you got fingerprints on your throat now?"

"Yeah."

"Damn."

"I know. Man, I've been looking at every black guy I've seen cross-eyed since the other night. This *has* to stop."

"Man—I can't say I blame you—but you gotta remember where you were and what you was doing at 3am. Black, white, green, you shouldn't a given a damn person a ride."

"I know."

"I know you know now. Don't do you much good though, does it?"

"Nope."

"Heheh. Man—I know you're cool with black people just like I'm cool with white people. You know it. You just gotta remember that motherfuckers are motherfuckers. There are plenty of white ones out there too."

"I know."

"Yeah."

"Hey listen—thanks."

"Man—that's what I'm here for. You want a cigarette?"

"Yeah, thanks."

"Let's go out on the porch…"

It's a clear night.

If this were bad poetry or a Celine Dion song, I'd say something encouraging about every man and woman living under the same sky. But it's not.

....

If this were a Corey Feldman movie, I'd be in class the next day wearing dark sunglasses and slouching. I do tend to slouch quite a bit, but no one notices the bruises on my face—or if they do, they don't have a visible reaction.

The teacher's talking about the intricacies involved in Marxist communism. He's so excited he's spitting. His beady little eyes are stretched open and magnified to absurd proportions behind those giant glasses.

The people in the front row are all scowling at having been spit on. The people in the back are all asleep. The only ones paying attention are the ones who already agree with him.

I'm drifting in and out of sleep.

The teacher starts laughing about how *ridiculous* it is that all governments aren't communist. He draws impressive diagrams on the chalkboard to prove his point. And he talks and he spits and he carries his bloated little body back and forth across the front of the room.

Finally, I can't stand it anymore. I raise my hand.

"But don't you think that communism stifles creativity and ingenuity?"

"How so?"

"Well—if you eliminate competition within the market place, doesn't that destroy the push for variation

and improvement? Wouldn't everything be generic?
Wouldn't art die without alienation, competition, or
distinction?"

"No no no. I think you're forgetting that Marx
was a poet, and..."

"And Hitler was a painter..."

The classroom is quiet.

....

I lie in bed staring at the ceiling. Cassandra
comforts me.

"Charlie—you're a nice guy. You treat people
pretty well. You just shouldn't be so hard on yourself.
Why don't you try smiling more?"

There's a dent in my ceiling in the shape of
James Christopher. The dent has two legs and an L-
shaped body. I match the outline to Cassandra's watery
curves.

The phone rings.

....

It's Sunday. Midday now. I'm sitting on the
porch of a house on one of those long streets unique to
poverty smoking a cigarette, half in the shade and half
in the sun. Across the street five young boys wrestle on
an old mattress in the yard. They bounce about and
shout and laugh as their bodies flip and contort in odd
mock wrestling moves.

I am twenty-two, if age even matters anymore.
I used to think there must be some sort of vitality
associated with youth—but really, it's all in the head. In
a low mood, my bones ache and hesitate. And
conversely, in high spirits I can bound and bounce and

shout and laugh and contort like the kids across the street.

·········

Through the lowest parts of the window you can see Ethan standing in the garage like a contemplative wallflower over a large and mostly blank canvas. Six pink fetal shapes stare back at him. I walk around to the rear of the garage and open the door. Inside are several garbage cans and recycling bins, planks of chipped wood propped up over boxes of discarded clothes amid piles of old forgotten hammers and electric screwdrivers, and a small table adorned with a portable cd player.

I unload a paper bag of beer onto a wooden shop table and throw one at Ethan, grinning. He is fixed between the small stereo and the canvas, which takes up half the length of the wall.

"How's your neck?"

"It's better. How about you?"

"I'm—"

"I know. It's a tough question."

"I guess."

"Well don't trouble yourself over it too much."

"No—I—I'm alright. I guess I've just been feeling a little stifled lately."

"It happens."

For a while I hang out the door rehashing the day over chains of cigarettes held and exhaled into the backyard.

And then some light bulb breaks, and Ethan disappears inside in a dash.

After a few minutes of rummaging, he resurfaces with an old typewriter and a stack of wrinkled white paper. We carry a picnic table to a nearby power outlet and invent an ashtray. And Ethan, inside, puts on a Satie record and returns to his fetal streaks.

I start typing as fast as my fingers can render a thought. It's past three am and clear above. I write things like, *"stars and alibis…where I ended blinking days in the backyard…or half forgotten dreams…or girls in old movies made in my mind…where the air is the opposite of smoke…"*. And, *"a hundred unopened umbrellas…or patchwork painters pretending to be heroes…or myself pretending to be religious on the garage floor…looking up at my bending mind as if some prize….or some important bag of wheat…"*

Inside, Ethan adds an odd green color to the pink fetuses, followed by several streaks of orange applied in broad bold strokes.

We break for a while to smoke dope and drink tequila on the cold concrete floor. Ethan jumps up periodically to add little dashes from a pool of grey paint that becomes the suggestion of mountains.

Meanwhile, I dash out to write a poem and then back to black out for five minutes on the cold floor. A minute later I wake up a little startled, get another idea, run out, then fall back in to black out.

Finally, I decide that food might prevent death. I manage enough energy to fry onions and garlic and diced tomatoes into three eggs, bits from a block of brie, a dash of (soy) milk, salt, pepper, chili powder, red pepper, and bacon bits.

I sit on the floor watching Ethan paint, and I think about Grace. I think about rushing in, and the fear in her, and all my attempts to assuage the fear. I want to tell her that I believe in freedom, or that I was happy being that ephemeral kiss goodnight.

I stumble out to the typewriter and hammer out, key by key:

i think i might go to sleep while it's still dark
i think i might drive away while limbs are still able to press
pedals
i think i might travel while the world still spins
i think i might grin as long as i have teeth
i think i might look as long as there are shapes for sounds
or realize while there are still colors
or the other way around—

i think i might type as long as i have fingers
or as long as the clicking creates cricket harmonies
as the moisture of the day is sweated out in the cold
or the silence speaks volumes that words could never penetrate
or that are simply slept off
and woken up with like secret mints under a well-used pillow

i think i might start a band and build a house and marry a
woman
and wash the dishes and clean the lint filter
and mind the children and tiptoe the solitude
and filter the personalities of bed sheets
and disguise the hair curlers as mysteries
and forgive the cotton underneath that was once silk
and the coarseness that was once mysteriously smooth
and the conversations that were once smoothly mysterious
and the love letters that were once automatic
like the mailman, or like the silences that meant something
or the windows worth daydreaming
or the pictures worth possessing
that carried a smell and a taste along with an image
and a moment along with an image
that never wanted a mantelpiece so much as a field to grow in
or so much as the sunlight that came with freedom
and the first sun that meant you were whole
that you thought i was threatening to block out

when really i only wanted to stand in your shade
when really i only wanted the taste and the smell
and never the image carved into stone that could become
threatening as they evolved into cotton and coarseness
and clothes lines and day jobs
and strained carrots and playgrounds where you stood by
with a pocketbook instead of a kite or a shovel
and a cigarette instead of a rose
and really i only wanted a garden
and the time it took to develop roses
and the rain that is natural
that you thought i might discontinue or interrupt
for a sunroom or an office space
or canned peas and a playground no longer yours--

no, i--
i only wanted to be the merry go round
that spun whenever you needed spinning
i only wanted the daylight as long as it felt like shinning
for the night is natural and inescapable
i only wanted those moments before the dusk swept you away
before we have to face the morning and the inevitability of curling
irons
and office shoes and neckties
and the responsibility beyond making you spin--

      I rip out that last page and gather the twelve
others strewn about the table, and I say goodbye to
Ethan and his newly polychromatic islands of paint.
And I drive home somehow quieted of life's casualties
by the hum and clang of an old machine and the time it
took to make it sing.

          ....

I tried aloof. I tried romance, tried balconies and guitars, tried stone faces and porch flowers, gargoyles and soft parades, allegories and direct admissions of admiration. I tried every angle on every angel. I tried starvation and suffocation, drought and rain, canyon and air, space and company...

I look Cassandra in the eyes. They are white and seemingly endless. I reach out to see. I pull them out and look at the caverns I created. I'm not even all that surprised that her insides are nothing but wires and metal.

And I was someone to whom she wouldn't have been compelled to speak. I was someone who stood in the corner often. I was someone who wrote frequently, and without realizing, the prose equivalent of a death rattle. I was someone who stared at screens and imagined eyes, skin, streaks of hair, a scent, the sound of air, a shadow on my bedroom wall. I was someone who spent too much time remembering shadows in the bedroom. I was someone who you would have passed if not for the eyes that everyone always said were old.

How did I end up here, hovering over you?

Where is pretty perturbed?

chapter fifteen:

A S h o w A b o u t N o t h i n g .

When the film ends, I stand up and walk out the emergency exit that leads to a pure white hallway. This is what heaven would look like if Stanley Kubrick was directing the afterlife.

Outside, the rain is coming down hard, and the sky is straight black as far as the eye can see. I stand under a little concrete canopy and light a cigarette while everyone else exits to their cars.

Young men hold young women's hands. Old women hold umbrellas. Old men hold umbrellas. No one else is trying to light a fire in the rain.

In the car I don't think about the movie so much as I do the young men and women. I was once a young man holding a young girl's hand. I used to buy the ticket and the popcorn. I used to watch them while they bought shoes and tried on expensive polyester skirts. I used to buy them flowers at grocery stores and gas stations. I used to take them to dinner at quiet Italian restaurants. I used to spend a lot of money on a lot of women. But those aren't the times I remember best.

I remember roof tops and secret meetings on school nights. I remember staying up all night crumpling paper until I found the right words. I remember gestures, sunrises, cloud patterns, first kisses, dumb fun, cheap fun, swing sets past midnight, beaches in November, pet shop kittens, and newspaper swans. I remember black and white movies on cable starring Audrey Hepburn and Gregory Peck. I remember sitting on a bed and playing guitar while a single candle sheds light over a nearby linoleum floor. I remember tufts of hair and nervous hands. I remember romances that lasted as long as matches but still burned brighter than the months spent with half-loves, or three-quarter muses.

Streetlights shine against the road until I'm not sure there's even a road anymore. I peer through the fogging glass to catch the yellow.

At home it is quiet, desolate, unforgiving. The rain dances on the roof with the wind.

And all I can think about is dancing.

....

Seasons come and go. Holidays roll by.

Children wearing orange plastic bags and white sheets knock on our door while their parents stand skeptically in our yard. I wonder if they can see the year's worth of cigarettes hiding behind the bushes.

Soon enough I'll be sitting at a table full of cranberries, sweet potato casseroles, silver chalices of gravy, golden plates of auburn turkey breast, mashed this, diced, broiled, strained that, garlic scented, herb roasted, marshmallowed, honey-glazed—

I always think of Thanksgiving and Christmas as days away from school, as congested traffic and crowded shopping malls, and as the beginnings of cold and flu season. I think of having to face relatives I've avoided all year. I think of what relative it makes more sense to satisfy with which visit. I am the strategic holiday. It's become like balancing a checkbook, or paying taxes.

....

Two brothers watch 22 men collide on plastic grass. The women meanwhile circle the adjacent linoleum, stewing a thousand things in a thousand pots, filling the room with the stereotypical holiday small talk. How long have we been doing this? No word from the crowd. No remembrance.

I remember little of this when I was a child. Only the outline sticks. I remember father #2, mother #1, grandparents #4 and 5, and aunt #47. Grandmother made twelve pies for every guest, set ornate eggs on lemon-scented tabletops that looked like mirrors, and stood silent and serious in the kitchen, stewing.

Father #2 eats seconds, thirds, fourths. His merriness is so very primitive and genuine that it is almost endearing to see him swallow whole turkeys. But everyone except the cook stares at him as if he is being entirely rude.

Grandfather #3 leads the charge after into the living room for the projection-tv marathon. Women whisper in the kitchen while mopping up our brief celebratory mess. I always thought when I was older, I would understand.

Why does eggnog remind us of Jesus Christ? Or pumpkin pie of pioneers? Or used cars of dead presidents? Or plastic eggs of religion and death? The American family has become so intent on honoring tradition, that it's become blinded of its own messages. The American family is a ghost and I am its unhappy minister. I say a sad prayer for the American family and I turn over in its grave.

Soon the turkey will be let out. Its legs, unbound, will hang down like melancholy raindrops, their poor pear-shapes charred and sullen. And everyone will eat peacefully, everyone except my father, who always seems to devour a warm meal as if it was a thing never before seen. Somehow I miss those primal, Lestrygonian urges.

Maybe if my idealism sticks well on into adulthood, I can mend. Maybe there won't be any more uncomfortable guests reaching out into the cold air for secret cigarettes. Maybe we won't have to talk about the weather, or traffic. Maybe we'll eat seconds without guilt. Maybe I won't be alone in the wine. Maybe the lawn won't be decorated with swinging paper Saint Nick and sad turkeys with faded red chins. Maybe there'll be great Grecian statues on my rooftop, like in Paris. Maybe we'll have an Arthurian table and the spirit and freedom of our founders. Maybe we'll talk about Thomas Wolfe and the Velvet Underground. Maybe I'll end up ignoring everything completely and wander the town, searching for some meaning in the world. Maybe there's a reason "family" is a broken image.

Maybe I'll stay at home and send everyone greeting cards with pictures of cranberries and mashed potatoes. "Happy thanksgiving, yours from the Underground."

Maybe my Dostoyevsky dreams will soften. Maybe some great girl, father #2, and I will drink red wine and devour dead birds happily in honor of that evil man Columbus, or whoever it was that discovered America and fought the civil war and cured rheumatism and put bread in plastic bags. I have my eye on America anyway. Just maybe. There'll be peace and goodwill at my table.

··········

The house is so much quieter without Stephen and James. Able works until midnight every night, comes home, gets stoned, and falls asleep. Tim is always either working, or relentlessly pursuing every bar, gathering, or keg party he can get his hands on. He's always coming home at around 2am with some sad story about a near miss with a girl who ended up having a boyfriend, or a mother, or laundry, or a summer home on Mars.

I, meanwhile, have burned enough bridges to keep my world volume relatively low. I sit in my room watching stacks of Woody Allen movies and the eight hour BBC renditions of Dickens novels my grandfather has lent me. I love the way you can experience a relationship, a childhood, even a life condescended down to a matter of hours. My greatest moments have happened vicariously through films. I've been on the road with Hunter Thompson. I've seen frogs fall from the sky like rain. I've fought massive intergalactic battles in space. I've freed entire school districts from vicious totalitarian regimes through pirate radio and the power of punk rock. I've picked up the perfect cynical beauty in a bar, toured with the greatest rock and roll bands of every generation, and seen the Roman Empire rise and fall again and again. All without leaving the comforts of my bedroom.

I watch romantic comedies, tragicomedies, black comedies, and cult classics. I watch dramas, suspense, science fiction, bad horror, governmental conspiracies involving Julia Roberts, and everything directed by Cameron Crowe and Kevin Smith. Every film has a little bit of life in it. I suck the marrow out of each one. I inject every heartbreak into my arm. I feel every death, every kiss in the rain, and every bullet in every epic battle scene.

I keep a bottle of tequila by the bed. If no one's called by ten o'clock, I'm well into its neck, and beating on its belly. I like to think of it as golden fire. It makes every part of my body warm. It tingles and burns. It's an amber blaze in my mouth and a bronze inferno in my stomach. It keeps me company.

Sometimes I listen to records and watch the smoke from my cigarette twirl around my fingertips. I don't really know where else to go anymore. We have fourteen boat ramps, sixteen hotels, twenty shopping centers, and over sixty restaurants. I've been to every one of them.

....

In the twenty second year of Charlie's life, in the twelfth month, on the second day, the fountains of the great deep were broken up, and the windows of heaven were opened.

I don't know how long it rained. I've been inside for so very long waiting for it to stop. I don't even notice the sound anymore. It's like the white noise that is every noise. After a while, it becomes the normal background *hiss* of the world.

Tim and I sit on the porch watching the world fall in great beads from the white rim of the roof. We've got rivers growing in the front yard. Soon we'll all need boats just to go to the convenience store for smokes.

Tim stands quietly against the door wearing his red and blue polyester uniform, and staring off into the foamy streets.

"When is this going to stop?"

"The rain?"

"Everything. I'm so fucking tired of my moods."

"Why don't you go see someone?"

"I guess I will. I've been meaning to. I'm just so damned busy all the time." His left hand is clawing at his side again, and he seems like he's been shivering for days.

When he sits down, his legs shake like hummingbird wings. When he talks, his eyes tremble. He's serious. I don't think I've ever seen anyone look more serious.

"I need help Charlie. I can't keep going on like this."

"I know Tim. I know."

chapter sixteen:

A f t e r   t h e   F l o o d .

And the brethren of Fell that went forth, were:

Able who slept with Eve: he began to be a mighty one in the earth.

Will who slept with Delia who slept with Stephen who slept with Althea who slept with Sid.

Simeon who slept with Crystal who was mad at Charlie for not sleeping with her.

Isaac who slept with Althea's former roommate who slept with Able.

Lola who slept with Charlie's former roommate who slept with Joan with slept with Dean.

Dean who slept with everyone and then slept with Joan again.

Henry who slept with Luna who slept with everyone.

Grace who slept with Henry's guitar player who was Charlie four years ago.

Stephen, abroad, who slept with Cassandra's exboyfriend's cousin.

Ethan who went with an old flame for as many times as the moon circles the earth circling the sun.

Timothy who went to a doctor and got a pill bottle of solutions.

Lamont who sold bags full of solutions.

Nigel, James Christopher, James Watson, and Jude who have known the bottle and the bag for as long as the moon has circled the earth circling the sun.

And everyone moved, like a great community of birds, back and forth between the same relative locations.

These are the brethren of Charlie Fell. This is the great American small town.

Charlie's Drunkenness

And Charlie planted a vineyard: and he drank of the wine, and was drunken; and he was uncovered within his tent.

And Eve saw the nakedness of her brother, and told his two brethren without.

And Tim and Able took a garment, and laid it upon both their shoulders, and went backward, and covered the nakedness of their brother; and their faces were backward, and they saw not their brother's nakedness.

Cigarettes and Sweethearts.

The college is quiet at night. I walk over the old cobble stone, past the hills of grass that were chairs during the day, under the streetlamps that have just woken up, and through the columns of pretend marble. A fountain springs the same water back and forth. I want to shatter its walls and let the little stream escape.

A half-painted wall stretches a hundred yards. Its archaic characters are the accumulated memory of the college. They begin a century ago and progress, through generations of war and civil rights. But the colors run out at the end of the seventies.

At the end of the wall is a park bench. And on the park bench is a girl.

"Audrey?" Her eyes study the cracks at her feet. In them a few little blades of grass break through. She looks up.

"Charlie? Hey."

"You remember me."

"Vaguely…"

"What are you doing out here in the middle of the night?"

"I don't know. I just had to get out of that room. I don't really know why sometimes. I just do."

We walk for a while under the streetlamps that have just woken up.

··········

Timothy Lloyd stands in the doorway. He's grinning a little. I wonder if the world is still so warm.

"Can I come in?"

"Yeah. Yeah." I lean up from the bed. "What time is it?"

"About eight. I just got off of work."

"Yeah. I guess I just dozed off. What's up? Why are you smiling?"

"I kind of—saw this girl again last night."

"Oh yeah? I take it it went well?"

"Yeah. I think so. We just talked for a while. But I think I'm going to see her again tonight. And she—she kissed me—or I kissed her, I don't know. It was raining and—I don't know. I really like this one, Charlie."

··········

I see Audrey again a few nights later. She comes over after class and launches immediately into an eight-minute rant on how all her roommates are driving her crazy. I hand her a beer and watch her body language personify each scene in incredible comic detail. Her hands are serious. They flap like exited wings at her every word, or like a cat with a piece of tape stuck to its paw. Her facial expressions are manic, disappointed, solemn, bitter, confused, and submissive. She's complaining and laughing at the same time. I hand her another beer and teach her how to jump up and down on a bed with a low ceiling.

When we catch our breath, she continues.

"God—they require so much attention. I love them, but—it's like I'm not there half the time."

"I know. They're all so busy with each other. Everyone I know is busy with everyone else I know, and none of them seem to think about much else."

"I know!" She flaps her arms again. I think she might start to fly.

I start laughing. I don't know if I'm supposed to, but I can't help it. Audrey, in turn, acts out a bit from an old TV show.

"Isn't it great how funny I am?"

I fake a sneeze. "Plagiarist."

"Hey…" She shoves me a little. I nudge her in the side.

Able and Eve appear in the doorway and announce their plot to liberate food from Tim's place of employment. We pretend they're funny, and wish them well.

And then the house is empty.

Audrey and I are leaned against a wall watching television. I'm at that moment again.

I lean towards her and tilt my head sideways.

I'm an inch away. I'm looking up.

Audrey freezes.

We don't move for a few seconds. We don't speak. I back away. And then we both lean together.

And then she stops.

"Charlie—the door's open."

I close it.

And then I pause.

"You're not just doing this because you've had a few beers are you, because…"

She kisses me no.

And then I take off her glasses. A mirror, armor. And her eyes look so different without them. I'm not sure if any of this is real. I haven't been sure of anything lately. I kiss her again. I hope it is. It feels—

An hour later, I walk her to her car, barefoot and vulnerable. It seems strange to kiss her in the street, under that streetlamp. It comes off a little wrong. But I do it anyway.

....

Timothy Lloyd stands in the doorway. He's not grinning anymore.

"Can I come in?"

"Yeah—" His eyes don't belong to him anymore. They look like they might try to escape.

"What's going on?"

He takes a bottle out of his pocket, empties a single pill into his hand, and swallows it with a gulp of Sprite. I know he's doing this in front of me on purpose.

"I think *she*—some one told me *she* has *herpes*."

"Who told you that?"

"Her best friend's boyfriend. And Sid. And Isaac. And Jude."

"Oh…"

"Yeah. I don't know what to do. I don't know if I should ask her if it's true, or how I should react if it *is*, or how I could possibly bring anything up. I don't know. I don't even know what the fuck *herpes* is, really. I know I don't want it…"

"Yeah. Jesus. How sure are you that she…"

"Four people, man."

"Yeah. How many guys has she slept with?"

"One."

"Jesus."

"Yeah. Charlie?"

"Yeah?"

"I really liked this girl."

"I know."

··········

I wipe the grass stains off the phone.

"Hello, Audrey?"

"Yeah."

"Hey, it's Charlie. What are you doing?"

"Pretending to study. And I must say, it's going quite well. I opened the book and everything."

"Yeah? Sounds like a real blast. Hey, what are you doing later?"

"Oh, I don't know. Listen Charlie, about the other night…"

"Yeah?"

"I don't know. I think I may have opened a can of worms I'm not quite ready to deal with."

"A can of worms?"

"I didn't mean it like that. It's just—I don't know. I don't really know were I am right now. Really, I'm just trying to survive the semester. I've got three weeks left and I'm just trying to survive."

"What happened?"

"Do you really want the history?"

"Sure."

"…" "When I was a kid, I was pretty happy. I had a lot of friends and everything was pretty stable.

And then we moved around a little.

And then we moved around a little more. And then high school started, and I didn't know anyone. So I stood in a lot of corners. I was a pretty perturbed kid. And then—I met this really *nice* guy. And—he stuck around for a while. And sometimes I thought he might stick around forever. He didn't.

Then I was miserable for a long time.

Then I met this other really *nice* guy, and I thought he might stick around for a while. He didn't. Then I followed all of this with a series of immaculately bad decisions. And since then I've spent a lot of time in hiding. And I—I just don't think I'm ready for much of anything else—right now.

I really just need a friend now, Charlie. I'm sorry…"

....

My friend Guinevere died in high school. I'd known her for years, and when she died, she was dating my best friend Tom. No one found out that she'd killed herself until the next morning at school. They actually broadcast it over the intercom during the morning announcements. I was in the bathroom at the time, downing a small container of gin. So I didn't hear the announcement.

Between third and forth period, I ran into a friend in the hallway who looked pretty bent out of shape about something. I asked him, "what's wrong man? You look like someone just *died*."

The friend, understandably, damn near socked me in the face. But after I managed to convince him of my ignorance, he took a deep breath and explained everything. And I went white.

For the rest of the day, a small group of us gathered in the music room, took deep breaths, and retained our pallid complexions.

It's hard to explain the feeling you get the first time you experience a death directly. Take the first time you've had your heartbroken, suck out all the air you have left, tie it to a thousand metaphysical questions, and add the situation of all your friends having their heart broken simultaneously. Then multiply the whole thing by twelve.

For a while, Tom went a little crazy. This is altogether understandable, being that he was on the phone with the girl when the gun went off.

But eventually he got his shit together. He took to pills, therapists and a number of new girlfriends. And now I see him every once in while, smiling damn close to that same crooked smile he's had his whole life, leaning out of a polished pick-up truck blasting the Sex Pistols.

Tom lived. Tom recovered.

The rest of us lived and recovered as well. We got our air back. We got our color. We survived.

Before Audrey, I don't think I've ever had my heart broken in a day.

There's a dent in my ceiling in the shape of James Christopher. The dent has two legs and an L-shaped body.

I'm staring at the walls again, I know. And my life isn't the greatest it's ever been, by any means. I think I went through the last decent woman in town the other night. It seems like I haven't had a job in a decade. All my friends are either disappearing, or else becoming catatonic on pills.

Sometimes my heartbeat seems a little off. Sometimes I think the pains in my chest are real. Sometimes I think thinking about the pains in my chest could make them real. Sometimes I think about this for hours.

But—then I think—if my heart could break, it would have done so by now.

....

The grass is drenched in cellophane, cigarettes, beer cans, braches, bank receipts, newspapers, shopping carts, catalogues, phone books, and dandelions.

I pull the plastic off of a fresh pack of smokes, and light two at once, not wanting to fall behind. It's funny how cigarettes express every emotion. They go well with company, in a bar rambling, or on the front porch with a crowd of friends sitting indian-style in the yard. Cigarettes go well after a meal and a lover, keep you company under a streetlamp, or linger in your hands when there is no one—

Cigarettes go with confusion. They can soften weak hearts, or dwell in slow puffs the same way a good feeling will when only just past.

Cigarettes are the best poets.

The other night I dreamt of being in a planetarium. I was looking up at the constellations overhead that weren't like any patterns I'd ever seen. And then I realized that we weren't looking at stars at all.

I looked dryly at my father who had grown slowly grey over the evening. He glanced down at his fingers that had started to hiss.

And then the sound grew louder. And then his fingers broke open, and there was something coarse and black underneath.

And then everyone's fingers snapped, and underneath their skin was something sinister and spider-like. And the sound of the hissing enveloped me. It was the sound made in movies for monsters, or for insects in high numbers on summer evenings.

Then whole crowd changed. They all grew coarse black hair and thin limbs. And the hissing projected from their eight thousand glass eyes. The hissing filled the air completely until there was no more room for sound. And then I looked down at my own fingers, which snapped just as I stood awake.

A little spider dangles dryly from a web to my right. I shiver a little and stand up.

Cigarettes and sweethearts can burn out. I light a match and think how valuable is a little fire.

....

Professor Rauschenberg passes out the last pages of the last test of the year. Eve and I scribble through it like two desperately racing greyhounds. The class doesn't matter anymore. The class hasn't mattered in months. The only thing we're aware of, is the fact that our time is about to become ours again.

The concrete walls in the hallway are suspiciously covered with paintings by people who have disappeared. One in a high corner is signed *Lola*

235

Thomas. I never see her face, but I see her brush strokes.

On the opposite wall is a sketch of a woman's profile done by an old drummer. Below it is a still life painted by a girl who used to borrow books from me. Now I see her shadow in bars, walking away.

Eve says goodbye in the parking lot. I walk away through the fake marble columns heading into the administrative building.

Audrey walks out of my English professor's office.
"Hey—can you hold on a second?"
"Sure."

Indiana Jones's father leans over a large pile of papers.
"Charlie—umm—I think it's over here. No. Here. Yes. Was this it?"
"Yeah, thanks."
"Okay. See you around."

"What's that?" I hand Audrey a bundle of paper covered in red remarks. She wrinkles her forehead. Through the glasses she looks like a highly determined elementary school teacher—but the kind of highly determined elementary school teacher that was striking enough that you'd do anything she ever asked without ever really knowing why.
She reads:

"You have a very interesting draft and a crew of renegade characters. You have a real facility for scenic compression, but you don't want to compress so much that the scene is obscured. Generally, you overdo exposition. You need to have more direct

action to support the narrator's analysis. You also leave a bit too much to conjecture. You need to reconsider some of your tactical uses of sentence fragment. You want to control the rhythm of your syntax. This is strong work. You're at a point where you can work on controlling details."

"Not bad."

"No. But you need to work on controlling the details, Charlie."

We're walking down the stairs. The hallways in between have no decorations. Now I'm not quite sure where I am at all.

"Do you need a ride anywhere?"

"No. No, I'm going back to the dorm. I've got two tests tomorrow and one on Thursday. Actually, I really have no business being out in public at all."

"Yeah. Well, uh—it was good seeing you. And—good luck on the finals."

"It was good seeing you too. Goodbye Charlie."

....

Ethan pours black and tans over a spoon bent to a 90-degree angle.

"Is that my favorite fucking spoon?"

"I don't know, man. It was in the drawer."

"Man, that was a great spoon. I've had that thing forever. We had some good times."

"Do you want this done right or not?"

"Aww—you broke the handle…"

"You're living in the past."

"I'm defending my cutlery!"

"Here—drink this and shut the hell up!"

Henry and Tim walk in the room.

"Hey Henry—didn't you have four papers to write tonight?"

"Yep."

"Beer?"

"Yep."

Ethan searches his bag for obscure jazz records. Tim lights up a joint. I take two drags and pass it to Ethan.

"Do you remember those joints you rolled the other night?"

"What about `em?"

"They were fucking terrible."

"They served their purpose."

(Laughing) "They fell apart in your hand. It was like eating wet sandwiches."

"Well, I think it might have had something to do with those awful papers …"

"Those were some *awful* papers…"

"Yeah, well—I mean—I didn't think I was hanging out with any *weed purists* or anything. I don't know. Sometimes you have to eat the peanut without even taking off the shell."

. . . .

What is it to love and not be loved? Is this, after all, the essential American experience? Has the freedom finally gone to our heads? Has the forest negated the trees?

I sit silently in a room full of women watching Meg Ryan movies. They're tearing up because Tom Hanks has happened upon the empire state building.

Their tear ducts swear their oath to romanticism. But their conditioning is bound to barflies and the circadian rhythm of mistakes. I don't know what to do or say anymore. I could treat them like garbage, win their tattered hearts and nurse them back to health. But I once I've abused them enough to win their affection, they'll have lost mine. No one falls in love with their own whipping boy.

I could "hang in there" and hope goodness comes back in style.

I could take to a more sinister set. I could play opposites and become beleaguered by nihilists. I could shave my head and climb a mountain. I could become one with the mountain lion and the billy goat. I could feed off of God's moss and Mother Nature's mountain air. I could die there alone; wondering was on television last Thursday.

I could take to chloroform and opium. I could rest out my troubles in a walking coma. I could poison my liver and steal David Crosby's. I could sell my possessions and take to some romantic hallway were time is like the peeling paint on the wall.

All my options feel like giving up. But I really can't think of an alternative. Is this, after all, the essential American experience? Has the freedom finally gone to our heads? Are we negating the flowers on our doorstep for the stars in the sky? I did that. I gave away the lover in my bed for the thousands in my head. And now, I am justly alone.

The Last Weird Mystery.

The phone rings. I fish it out of the sink.

"Charlie—hey, it's Audrey. Are you doing anything?"

"Not really."

"Do you mind if I stop by for a little while?"

"Yeah. Yeah, sure…"

"Great. I'll see you soon."

Audrey opens the door and walks in.

....

"How were the exams?"

"Oh wonderful. I mean, if you enjoy acupuncture with steak knives."

"I can't say that I do."

"Yeah…"

She hands me a bar of red translucent soap with a candy cane floating in its middle. "I made like a hundred of these, so…"

"Thanks."

"Yeah…"

"Do you want a beer?"

"Yes."

We're sitting on the bed again. The television is on. The door is open.

We fast forward through the commercials, wade through the static on the tape, and laugh despite the many mechanical distractions.

And then I kiss her. And it's like a summer tan and a winter windburn.

And she holds on a little tighter.

And I'm not trying to swim this time. This time I've given into floating. If the ocean wants me deep, I'll go deep. If it wants to cast me back onto the shore, I will go back.

She holds on a little tighter this time. She pulls my hands to hers, and lies beside me. She's almost comfortable enough to sleep. She closes her eyes—

There's a dent in my ceiling in the shape of James Christopher. I live on that ceiling. It's white and blank save for the shape of a man. But I stopped seeing the drunk who fell down a long time ago. Now I see a nameless man standing on a blank page. Now I think about all the colors that could be drawn, and all the spaces that have yet to be filled. Now I see a story that's screaming to be born.

Woman is the best company. Woman goes well in a bar rambling, or on the front porch with a crowd of friends sitting indian-style in the yard. Woman keeps you company under streetlamps, or lingers in your hands when there is no one else—

I remember the first girl who laid her head in my lap, and how her hair smelled. I remember climbing on rooftops to look at the stars. I remember wanting to jump so much.

I remember being caught, and I can still feel being dropped.

But I'm here again. I'm sitting on the shoreline. There's a girl beside me. Her breath is like the hum of the ocean. It flows in and out. It carries with it meaning and sand, history, life, and death.

I reach for a blanket.

"You can't cover an ocean, Charlie."

"What?"
"I should go."
"I know..."

"Charlie—I'm going home tomorrow."

"I know. I'll walk you out."

"Charlie?"

"Yeah?"

"Thank you."

....

I wake up early on Christmas morning. The world is enveloped in a thin layer of frost. All the cars are covered in sharp crystalline stars, and even the road is coated in a thin black sheet.

At mother's house, a small child swims in a shimmering sea of emerald wrapping paper, burgundy bows, and silver foil. He smiles wordlessly and topples over into the soft piles.

I sit on the floor sipping hot coffee and staring at the decorative branches that were once apartment complexes. Plastic apples hang from metal wires where once a family of birds nested, or a squirrel paused. I almost can see its nose twitching in the cold as his bright black eyes beam curiously.

We used to have cats that batted gleefully at the plastic apples. Mother would scold them with hisses and verbal threats, but their eyes just twinkled innocently, picking up the soft gleam of Christmas lights.

Mother walks back and forth between the kitchen and the living room in a new white bathrobe. She brings us platefuls of strong-smelling breakfast sweets strung with white icing. I take a bite of cinnamon, cake, apple, raisin—

And then the little toddler tackles me, and hands me a fistful of ribbon.   His father laughs from his leather chair while mother, exhausted, curls up on the floor in a plush new sleeping bag.

At my father's house two children wrestle for supremacy of butterfly nets. The older is determinedly poised and the younger is a kicking maniac. Their mother runs interference while father takes deep, amused breaths and rolls his eyes knowingly.

He's sitting at the piano now, disconnected from his body, the bookshelf to his left, and the large synthetic tree decorated in plastic picture frames and tangles of silver to his right. His fingers wander the keys like blind serpents. They hear something—some accident—and run backwards looking for it.

The children are tearing apart simple microscopes, plastic mansions, dinosaurs, books, jackets, and mouthfuls of chocolate.

I sit in the corner hoarding my own boxes, hoping they can't see me behind all the sugar.

Outside, an old cat stretches in the few and fleeting patches of sun that grace the short wooden porch.

At grandmother's apartment we are refined and jovial on comfortable furniture.

Years ago all this—the rugs, couches, cookware, cabinets, coasters, chairs, tables, trays, televisions, photographs, and paintings, were strewn about in a massive house on the river. Now everything is condensed and cozy. The fake fireplace is gone. The Christmas tree is streamlined, and where once a lengthy table stretched just inside the front door, is a narrow hallway and small coffee table for coats and keys.

But life is sort of like that. When you're young, the world is infinite and expanding. You want your legs to stretch, and your eyes to conceive and wander. You need all the room possible. As you grow older, you begin take those relics out of experience and condense them in an ever-smaller setting.

Now all those memories are stacked neatly in a large oak cabinet in the living room.

Grandmother feeds everyone nicely spiked eggnog while grandfather flips through football games and reminds his youngest grandson of a nearby plate of frosted sugar cookies.

At dinner we indulge in tender beef, crisp biscuits, soggy salads, sliced potatoes, and slick green beans. And it's so quiet you can almost hear the candles flickering.

Afterwards the guests engage in social arguments while grandmother scrubs, and grandfather flips through football games and reminds his youngest grandson of a nearby plate of frosted sugar cookies. Through a glass door, a balcony overlooks a slender river and the lights that line its shore. It's peaceful and cold outside, and I think what oddly regular partners those two are.

Between football games, there's a video of a man sitting peacefully on the floor, explaining how he executed his plan to kill a skyscraper full of Americans. *"We brought them to their knees,"* he says as we watch him creep in his cave on our wide-screen television with full bellies and a floor full of wrapping paper.

....

At home I unravel on the floor amid a sea of emerald wrapping paper, burgundy bows, and silver foil.

Timothy Lloyd stands in the doorway. His eyes look black and glassy like my imaginary squirrel.

"How was Christmas, Charlie?"

"Tiring. You?"

"Pretty much the same."

"What's going on tonight?"

"I think I'm going to Sid's in a little while. You're welcome to come."

"Do they have anything to drink?"

"I'm sure…"

"Sounds great."

Sid, Isaac, Eve, Able, Henry and Jude are strewn about the living room like so much wrapping paper. Henry and Jude talk about a band they were in during high school.

Sid and Tim talk about a band they were in during high school.

Eve and Able talk about a band Sid and Tim were in during high school.

A blonde girl walks through the door. She's not very interesting looking. Her face is sort of plain and round. Her features are arranged like an unimaginative still life. Henry and Jude went to high school with her.

I'm a year older than everyone else in the room. Everyone I went to high school with has moved and had two children, six jobs, three divorces, fourteen fences, eighty addictions, and an innumerable amount of lawnmowers, mailboxes, backyards, therapists, plumbers, and haircuts. I haven't had a good haircut in a while.

Eventually everyone filters into Isaac's room. A poster on the wall reads,

Marijuana—at least it's better than crack.

Everyone is reciting names.
"Have you seen Watson lately?"
"Remember Rose?"
"God—I ran into Casey on Tuesday…"
"Christopher…"
"Saturn…"
"Jupiter…"
"Mars…"
"Winter…"
"Spring…"
"Summer…"
"Fall…"
"Fell…"
"Fell? Fell—are you alright? Fell?"

There's no shape in this ceiling. There's no body. There are no legs. It's all just blank.

I stand up and walk out. I walk out the door and run down the stairs. I run through the front door and down the street. I turn left and then right. It's cold outside. And yet, it's oddly peaceful.

I run across the highway and down one of those endlessly stretching streets unique to the small town lower class. I run by the chain link fence of the middle school where I used to run the mile in 6:04. The gate is open, but no one is there.

My lungs hurt a little. Images of everyone I've ever known are dancing on my unborn grave.

I hit the front yard. The grass is covered in cobwebs of frost. My streetlight is burnt out.

I am in the street now looking down the open length of road that runs through the horizon. I am in the street thinking how far this life does stretch, and what little courage it would take to walk.